My House Is Full of Whispers

My House Is Full of Whispers
Copyright © 2014 by Wendy Rathbone
and Eye Scry Publications.

Eye Scry Publications
www.eyescry.com/html/publications.htm

ISBN 13 # 978-0-9896938-6-8
TITLE: My House Is Full of Whispers
Author: Wendy Rathbone

Address all inquiries to the author at: wrathbone@juno.com

Description: *Ten erotica short stories by Wendy Rathbone. Leda has not one beautiful man, but two. Kale enters a secret world in a wealthy man's basement. Noah is in love with a man who hates sex. Dina lives next door to a famous Hollywood director she secretly loves. Dorian has a sixteen year old female student coming onto him. Tara is haunted by an erotic ghost. Young Dimitri is kidnapped by lecherous men. And more.*

My House Is Full of Whispers

by

Wendy Rathbone

A Collection
of
10 Erotic Stories

*"Writing erotica became a road to sainthood
rather than debauchery."*
-- Anais Nin

Table of Contents

Author's Preface

When I wrote these stories, I deliberately set out to gently break down certain barriers, and I've certainly broken taboos. Do I care? No. This is fantasy at its purest level. The stories are never meant to be political statements, nor do they make any attempt at political correctness, and there is little consideration for safe sex. While I definitely condone safe sex, my stories come from fictional realities in my head where safe sex is not much of a concern because, well, it's imaginary and it's *fiction*!

For me, these stories are meant as little poetic erotic ramblings merely to stir the flames of desire, nothing more. They are pure fantasy and therefore to be enjoyed as such. Every story is erotic in nature, meant to titillate, some more explicit than others. Some of the stories are light, some are darker. I invite the reader to a feast of diversity and delight.

*Heterotica * Male/Male * Menage*

Wendy Rathbone

Leda

*"We are three. The moon comes
from its quiet corner, puts a pitcher of water
down in the center. The circle
of surface flames.
One of us kneels to kiss the threshold.
One drinks with wine-flames playing over his face.
One watches the gathering
and says to any cold onlookers,
'this dance is the joy of existence'."*
                                                -Rumi

Pale light from the window gave Antonio's dark hair a bronze glaze. He squinted through the glare, smiling, and it was as if the air caressed him. Knees spread, torn jeans exposing sun-browned kneecaps, he was the most relaxed person in the room.

Rory made no move to hide the tremor in his hand as he reached for the tall thin glass of rum and coke Antonio had served him. He kept looking from Antonio, with the cryptic smile and sun-embraced skin, to Leda, the only woman in the room, and who was watching the whole scene through a warm peach wine-cooler haze. She'd had two already and was debating on starting her third but felt too good to get up and get it.

Leda had met the two men separately under somewhat unique circumstances. Rory, who had long golden hair and pale brown eyes, was definitely 'her type' and she had run into him in two different stores on two different days. The first time, in Vons, Rory had turned a corner blind and they collided. He picked up her armload of cat food and bowed. Leda was swept into instant infatuation and couldn't speak.

7

By the time she realized she should find out his name, he was half an aisle away, heading for the exit. His tight white pants and black t-shirt stung her inner eye with an image that haunted that night's dreams. The next day, in K-Mart, they smacked into each other again. She was ready. She'd engineered the whole thing. They introduced themselves. They dated twice. Nothing had happened between them. Yet.

Antonio, the more mysterious of the two, Leda met while jogging at sundown. He'd turned his ankle on a hill. She almost hadn't stopped as she approached, fear crouching inside her as it always did when she was not in a crowd, when she was alone, when she was with a stranger. But his black eyes seemed to call. The strangest thought entered her mind as she slowed. *The dark side of the moon speaks in silence and shadow. I can take you there. I can give you the enigma you seek.* She and he smiled at each other at the same time. It turned out he lived alone, only a block away from her, in a small white house. He liked to read Machiavelli and Goethe. He was twenty-eight and claimed to be a real estate investor. For no logical reason, Leda did not quite believe him.

Rory and Antonio also met by accident. Leda and Rory were at the local diner eating dinner. It was their second date. Antonio walked in with a darker man who followed him like a shadow, came over to their table and introduced himself. He invited them both to his house for drinks the following evening. They accepted.

Now they sat in Antonio's clean, white living room. Antonio's shadow-man was nowhere in sight. But Leda had suspected the night before, from the way the man had followed Antonio and bowed his head to him, acknowledged his every word, that they were more than friends. She had expected him to be with Antonio when they arrived.

Instead there were just the three of them. An odd number that always left an odd-man-out. It made her slightly uncomfortable, but at the same time euphoric. It wasn't too often that she had the company of two handsome gentlemen all to herself. The fact that she was physically attracted to both made it difficult to concentrate on much of what they said. Instead, conversation passed over her like the cooling currents of a summer stream. She breathed in slowly, then out. The air smelled of Antonio. Of myrrh.

Rory was still uncomfortable. Leda could see it in the way he sat, back straight, legs slightly spread but with both feet planted firmly on the floor. The wicker couch could have been a divan of nails for all the comfort it gave him.

She herself preferred the floor. She rested on her elbows against white carpet and black pillows and admired the wicker furniture and the pale wooden Venetian blinds. Antonio's décor was inspired. She told him so.

The sun had set. Through the half-closed blinds she could see a red sky, and bruises of purple where cloud fluffs reflected the waning light.

"It's perfect," she said.

"What?" Antonio asked.

"The sky."

Rory took a gulp of his drink. "Yeah." He grimaced when Antonio got up from his chair and leaned over him to peer out the window.

"Hey, that's magnificent." His voice was low, almost a whisper. Leda felt her skin heat. She saw Rory looking at the man's body up and down as Antonio continued to lean, to stare. Then Rory looked guiltily away.

Good, she thought. *They like each other. It's a start.*

The wine coolers were doing to her what they always did. Making her warm and open and wet in dark places, in secret corners and crevices. She'd always had fantasies of being with two men at the same time. But this wasn't a dream. Here were two men who had their own decisions to make, who had their own free wills.

She smiled.

"What's that smile for?" Antonio asked, stepping away from the couch and Rory.

Leda looked at her legs which were stretched before her, knees slightly bent, black skirt riding up one firm thigh. "For you," she answered.

"Me?" He pointed to himself. His white t-shirt stretched across his chest and he poked his forefinger between the two rounded, raised areas of his pectoral muscles. He looked like sculpted rock. It was obvious he worked out on a regular basis.

Leda nodded, then gazed at Rory. He was watching both of them, a little more relaxed now, she noticed. Since the attention was off him for the moment, he could afford the rest.

"I was just thinking about you in a certain way," Leda confessed. Boldness was a natural trait within her...when she felt safe. At another time, Antonio might have intimidated her. But not now. She could tell he liked her. That made her more secure.

"What way?" His hair, the bronze slowly bleeding out of it as the evening darkened, was like liquid onyx now.

"Without those," she said lazily, pointing.

He looked down at himself. "What?"

"Your clothes."

He paused, his lips curving slightly, the muscles beneath his eyes firming. The lashes made wing-like shadows on his cheeks. A gold bracelet flashed on his wrist as his hand slowly moved. Low voice drawing out the words, he said, "All right." The hand rose; the arm bent. He grasped the collar of his t-shirt and pulled it over his head. It was off in seconds. His bare chest gleamed, brown and hairless. Leda sat up. Rory looked at his lap.

Antonio ignored them. "You ask for it, you get it," he said to her stunned amazement. Long fingers began undoing the buttons of his torn jeans. She could only watch.

Rory let out a loud breath. Leda glanced at him, quickly glanced back. Antonio was going to do it! He was really going to strip!

10

When every button was undone and a flash of white briefs could be seen beneath, Antonio stopped. "Not fair," he said. "I'm not prepared to be the only one."

"Me?" Leda couldn't keep the disbelief from rising in her tone.

"You," Antonio said. "And you." He pointed to Rory.

Rory choked, coughed twice, raised both eyebrows and said, "Here?"

Antonio nodded.

Leda grinned and shrugged. "Okay." She had on a short cotton pull-over, a black skirt. She raised the shirt over his head and tossed it. Reaching between her breasts to the clasp of her black bra, she looked up. Both men were watching. As an audience they were appraising. She couldn't have done better. Secure in that, she unfastened the bra and draped it over her leg. She could feel her nipples instantly harden under the double male gaze. Her blood ran cold, then hot. Deep inside, her womb ached.

Antonio glanced at Rory. "Now you."

Rory had his drink in hand. He set it down, sloshing some of it onto the back of his hand. Leda and Antonio smiled but said nothing.

Without preamble, and with somewhat awkward innocence, he stripped off his black tank top. It was the same one he'd been wearing the day Leda had first bumped into him. It fell into a rumpled pile beside him on the white, wicker couch.

Rory had pale golden skin, and a fine sheen of golden hair that, instead of curly, was perfectly straight on the upper portions of his chest. He looked sprinkled in stardust. His belly was flat and quivering. Leda wanted to run her hands down it, but she didn't move.

"Ah." It was Antonio. He caught Rory's eye and winked. Rory turned a subtle shade of bronze.

Next, Antonio slid the torn denim from his long legs. Through the taut, white material of his underwear, Leda could see the roundness of his testicles and the point of a penis with the beginning of an erection. She held her breath, then let the air out slowly between her dry, parted lips.

Her turn came. The black skirt fell to her ankles and she kicked it away. Her black bikini panties, wet at the crotch, left little between her and the air.

Rory pushed his elastic-waisted, multi-colored pants to the floor. They looked like puddles of rainbows at his feet. He wore white Hanes, much like Antonio's. The bulge between his legs was somewhat smaller, but Leda suspected half of it was hidden between his now tightly clamped, naked thighs. He held his arms crossed in front of his chest.

"Last but not least..." Antonio snapped the waistband of his underwear.

Leda and Rory watched.

"No," he said suddenly. "I think you first." He turned to Rory.

Rory half-smiled and looked shyly away. "Why not all at the same time?" he asked desperately.

"All right," Antonio agreed. "But we have to make a pact first."

"What kind of pact?" Leda asked.

"That no one holds back. And that whatever happens afterward, happens with no regrets."

"I agree," Leda said, her breasts hardening with excitement, her body wet between her legs.

"I agree," Rory said hesitantly, without looking up.

"I agree," Antonio said, three fingers going under his waistband. "No turning back. No regrets."

They all nodded.

"Okay." His dark fingers pushed against the white of the cotton. A thatch of curly black hair showed, and a rectangle of pale brown skin.

Leda looked at Rory. His underwear was already pushed to his knees. The muscles of his flank flexed. His skin glowed amber.

12

Leda pushed her black panties gracefully to her ankles and looked up. Antonio's penis was just springing free. It dangled, half-hard, a dark shade of rose. Immediately, she wanted to touch it.

Rory cast the last of his clothing away. He leaned back on the couch and stared at Antonio. Against one thigh, his pink organ throbbed.

Still standing, Antonio was magnificent. Tight testicles supported the growing organ that looked as if it needed affection. Even Rory was magnetized by it. His gaze was like a statue's, dream-like and still.

No one moved.

"We have magic in this room," Antonio murmured.

It might have sounded ridiculous to say it at any other time. But this particular evening the words were perfect. "Yes," Leda whispered. The top of her head felt open, displaced. The room swam before her like a dream.

'Yes," Rory echoed.

Antonio was the first to move. Leda thought he would approach her. Instead, he went to Rory, who moved back slightly on the couch.

Antonio held out his hand. "No. Don't. It's all right. I think you're beautiful. And Leda's here. So I'm not a threat, am I?"

Rory swallowed hard.

Antonio stood directly in front of him. "Go on. Touch me. I know you want to. And I know it would turn Leda on."

As Rory shyly succumbed to the darker man's strange charm, Leda felt herself melting away. Her body was like wax. Her insides burned.

Rory reached out. His hand still shook. The tips of his fingers caressed in a downward stroke over Antonio's hip, the inner curve of muscle there, the straight-muscled thigh.

"Yes."

Rory looked up, eyebrows raised.

Antonio's cock thickened. "Yes, "he said again, quietly. "It's okay."

Rory's hand moved forward on the thigh, brushing down.

"It's okay, isn't it, Leda?" Antonio asked. "You like this, too, don't you?"

"So far it's been only in my dreams," she replied softly. Her skin quivered. The two men were so smoothly sculpted, so beautiful. "Until now."

"It's true," Antonio said softly to Rory. He reached out and touched the top of his head with his palm. Like a halo above Rory's head, his gold bracelet flashed. "There's nothing wrong here in anything we're doing. And I want you to touch me because I know you want to touch me."

Rory took a quick breath, blinked, swallowed again.

"Have you ever touched a man?" Antonio suddenly asked.

Rory shook his head.

"It's easy. And it's good. And Leda likes it. I like it. I know you'll like it. Let go, Rory. Let go of your inhibitions, golden boy." His fingertips combed through the pale, silken hair.

Rory closed his eyes and opened them. His lips pressed tightly together. He stared at Antonio's penis for many long seconds before his mouth finally relaxed, and his hand came back up. Now Antonio stroked his shoulder. His palm made a shushing sound against Rory's bare skin.

"Um." Antonio groaned. The insides of Rory's fingers brushed over his cock. "Take it," he ordered. "Please. Take it in your hands."

As if under a witching spell, Rory obeyed. His lips curved slightly. He seemed fascinated. Leda's body was on fire just watching.

Using both hands, Rory pulled gently on the throbbing erection, letting the slim hardness press against the curve of his palms. After a moment of that, of getting used to the feel, he began to stroke Antonio with long, firm pressure.

14

Antonio touched Rory on the shoulders, on the head. He ran his fingers through Rory's long hair, caressed his face. He moaned again, bowed his head, threw it back. His hips thrust. Rory held him tightly in his grip.

Leda could take no more. She got up and approached them, her body glowing, banked with heat. Gently, she took Antonio's penis from Rory's tight grip. "Like this," she said, and leaned forward and put her dry lips to the tip in a feather-light kiss. "Now you," she said.

Rory leaned forward, imitating the kiss. His lips touched the tip of Antonio's cock. It twitched.

"Yes, "Antonio hissed.

"And now like this," Leda said. She leaned forward, one hand holding the penis, the other pressed against his flank. She opened her mouth and licked the tip. It had the flavor of velvet and salt, the texture of warm plastic too long in the sun.

Rory imitated her, leaning forward and touching the penis-tip with his tongue.

"Now you wet your mouth," Leda said, forcing all her saliva toward her lips, "and do this." She enveloped the head of the cock with her lips. When she pulled back, the cock-head glistened.

Rory did the same. His mouth pursed against the thickness. His eyes closed, the lashes brushing his cheeks like soft pale fringe. Leda had never seen anything like it. Rory didn't pull off, but pushed his mouth further onto the erection. It was fiery to watch, exhilarating. Leda had the instant realization that there was nothing more tender or more fierce than watching a man suck another man, willingly, delicately, and enjoying what he was doing, loving it.

When Rory finally pulled off, flushed cheeks hollowing as he sucked, Leda took his place and sucked in the hard flesh. She loved doing this. And men loved it. The feel of a penis in her mouth, the ecstasy of giving in this way, made her dizzy. She sucked without swallowing, without using her teeth. She heard Antonio let out a noise like a broken sob. She came off him, leaving a trail of saliva, and said, "Too fast?"

"I love it," he said. "But I need to sit down."

Rory and Leda moved to opposite ends of the couch. Antonio sat between them, his gleaming erection jutting upwards. His black hair like spilled ink fell into his eyes. Shyly, Rory reached out and brushed it back. They grinned at each other like schoolboys before both turning to Leda. Antonio reached out and cupped her right breast. He ran one thumb over the nipple.

The skin on Leda's arms and legs became charged, shot through with the electrical impulses of pure pleasure. Antonio leaned down and brushed his lips over her breast, licked between them and kissed the other one. His mouth was a soft, warm pressure.

After a few seconds, he lifted his head. Their lips met in a kiss that opened her further. Her hand reached out and brushed his penis which was still firm and hot, still seeking release.

When they broke away, Leda saw Rory staring at her. She smiled and leaned across Antonio, her body beckoning him to her. Rory leaned in and they kissed while Antonio watched. Rory's heated mouth opened to Leda and their tongues met. Suddenly, another mouth intervened and they turned their faces to Antonio who kissed first Leda, then Rory, his hand curved against the back of his neck in a miniature embrace.

Antonio's leg against Leda's thigh was like flame. She leaned into him, gathering the energy of him against her body. Suddenly his head dropped and he licked Rory's penis. Rory gasped and fell back against the couch arm.

"Feel good?" Antonio dropped to the floor and knelt between his legs.

Rory closed his eyes until they were no more than thin lines of black on his taut face, and nodded.

Leda knelt, too. She watched as Antonio took Rory's entire length into his mouth, then pulled silently off it. Rory's

16

stomach muscles shuddered. His penis grew. Antonio repeated the gesture, his thumb and forefinger closing on the base to hold the organ in place. As he went down on it, she heard a soft suckling sound. Her own genitals throbbed. Antonio's free hand massaged the tight testicles.

Rory's breathing was labored. Yet he lay very still as Antonio continued to suck.

Her hands pushing against Antonio's thighs, Leda lay down on the floor and took his own darker penis into her mouth. When he felt her presence, his knees spread. She used her fingers to hold him and feasted. He grew even harder in her mouth. She tasted a salty sweetness, smelled the deep scent of musk, and let her lips catch against the ridge of the cockhead as she moved up, then back down again.

She no longer noticed the passage of time, nor the shadows darkening in the room. It was Rory's voice that finally startled her back to reality.

"Wait. Wait. I don't want to come yet!"

Leda looked up. Antonio was sitting back, lips wet and slightly parted. Rory's cock bulged upwards from his thatch of golden hair. It was thick with arousal, glistening. Rory's face looked rapt, his dark eyes wet with lust. "Oh god," he breathed.

"Are you sure" Antonio asked.

He nodded, breathing out.

The room had deepened to hues of beige and brown as full evening bloomed. It gave everything an eerie quality of unreality. Their bodies were dim shimmers of light.

"Leda's turn," Antonio whispered. His strong arms pulled Leda to him and he propelled her onto the couch beside Rory. Both men turned all attention onto her.

Rory sucked at her throat, her breasts. Antonio bent his head between her legs.

When his tongue first touched the folds of skin on her vulva, she almost cried out. With wet flicks, it delved deeper, finding moist crevices with its heat. Her head tossed from side to side.

Rory moved away from her. She lifted her head and saw him lie down on his back between Antonio's legs. There, between his legs, he took Antonio's cock in his mouth. The inspired gesture was quite a testament to Antonio's persuasive charisma since Rory had never done anything like this before with a man.

A little later, when Antonio entered her it was like having all the shackles of existence break away. She became enveloped in wind and warmth instead of skin. Light and darkness simultaneously took over her mind. Instead of blood, her body ran on an electrical current that quivered through it like laser lines of light. She was liquid and hard and broken and whole.

Antonio thrust.

Her breasts throbbed. He touched them.

Her lips stretched against her teeth. He kissed them.

Out of the dimness came Rory's cock bobbing in front of her. She licked it. She kissed it. She sucked it. Antonio bent forward, pushing in, out, in, and sucked it from her mouth into his. They traded turns with it until Rory cried out and Antonio sucked him down hard as he thrust into Leda. As Rory thrust into his mouth, Leda arched.

Rory came first. They used their hands and mouths to draw out every pearly drop of fluid he had to give.

Afterwards, Leda felt herself turned until she was on top of Antonio. Rory leaned between them and licked with quick, wet laps at the entrance to her body, at the exposed part of Antonio's cock.

Leda came second, gripping Antonio with her thighs and holding him still. He thrust hard as she came, stilled, then pulled out and, as Rory captured the head in his mouth, cried out and came.

Later, when the night rose like a wave of quiet gloom, when shadows peeked over pools of star and lamplight, when the moon rose full and fleshy in an aroused and dampened sky, they made love again.

And again.

Man From Another World

"But you were always there,
courting the favor of the shadows
perhaps guiding my steps toward the path
that might
one day
lead me back to you."

-Della Van Hise, *"Seven Year Blues"*

My house is full of whispers.

Doors rattle in the late evenings as if someone is passing through.

Scents of wild musk and myrrh cling to the dark air of the hallways.

Shadows move like men from room to room.

I knew there was someone else in my home the moment I moved in. Not someone from this world. And not a ghost. But someone from another place that occupied a space in another time, another reality.

My name is Tara. I'm twenty-four years old and I live alone.

I don't know if my house is special, or if, perhaps, many people encounter these beings from time to time and simply choose never to speak of them. But I tell this story as it happened and assure that every word is as true as the existence of the sun, the moon, the distant ache of stars.

First Encounter

On a gloomy February day I sat in my den with soft music like bells on wind playing as a background to my efforts to compose new poems.

My occupation as a poet as paid very few of my bills over the years but I rather ridiculously consider it, above all the other jobs I've held, my primary function as an individual upon this Earth, and my preferred title in life.

While struggling with notes and chaotic rough drafts of phrases that made no sense and offered only a drunken kind of pleasure to my thoughts, I leaned back and began to drift into a hazy doze.

A sharp noise startled me awake. The door knob at the entrance to the room clicked. I blinked, pushed back the hair from my eyes, and was astonished to find that the shiny, brass handle was moving.

The music still filtered through the air like a haunting echo, lending a macabre note to the event.

I held my breath and froze.

I could think of nothing to do but wait and watch.

For some unknown reason, I felt only shock, no danger. But my body was cold, and the suddenly too-close walls of the room seemed to heave.

The part of the mind that reasons was gone. My senses were heightened but, because of that, strangely desensitized to everything but my tunnel vision, and the sound of metal catching metal as the door handle moved.

A buzzing sounded in my ears. My lungs burned. Still, I held my breath.

The door knob glimmered, then stopped turning as though whoever stood on the other side held it still.

I waited.

After what seemed like minutes, the door swung inward so quickly it hit the side wall. The bang shattered the breath from my lungs. I inhaled with an audible gasp.

The hall was dark. I thought I saw a shadow move. Then there was nothing. No sound. No scent. No sign of anything but the open door swinging slowly closed now, and my elevated pulse.

I sat for a long time staring at the door. It had already swung forward halfway and stopped, and all I saw was the hall, the white wall beyond, and the gloom created from lack of light as if the day itself were captured in my house's shadows.

Second Encounter

After awhile, I got up. My body seemed frozen. My muscles and bones ached with a kind of cold that comes from deep despair, from loss.

I never for once thought my house was haunted. I believed that whatever had been outside my door had been real, and alive. But now for some reason it was gone. And I had no power to stop it from leaving, or to call it back.

I'm not a brave person, but I wasn't afraid. I was disturbed, however, by the cold, and by being startled awake. And I was disturbed that whoever it was hadn't let me see them.

I walked down the hall and into the bathroom. As I bent to draw myself a hot bath I thought I heard a sound. I turned. Something whispered past my ear. The language was hushed and inaudible. It was gone before I could be sure I'd heard anything at all.

Sighing, I threw in flower-scented bubble beads and ran the water until it steamed.

The white bathtub gleamed with steaming liquid slick with soap bubbles. It was like the embrace of a fantastic, sensuous creature as I entered its flowing warmth. My body warmed and relaxed against the slippery porcelain. Only my knees and head were above water now. I floated.

After awhile, of their own accord, my hands found the sensitive entrance to my body and began to probe, to stroke, to rub. My knees poked out of the water like light brown islands. The water lapped against them and the slick sides of the tub in soft splashes.

I'd left the door to the bathroom open. Now I let myself feel the pleasure of my hands, let my thoughts reach out, my fantasies pretend whatever I wished.

My visitor was a poet. A lover.

Watch me. I sent the message telepathically. *Watch me.* The mere thought of my visitor seeing me bathe and caress myself heightened the pleasure. I imagined he was male and very tall. I imagined his black hair was long and hid one eye in an artful curl as he stood in darkness and winter, cold and alone, lonely and lost, watching me, wanting me.

What is your name? I asked. My body arched. *Why are you here? I want you. I want you. I want you.*

My muscles clutched my middle finger in a strong orgasm that lasted until the water cooled and my skin shriveled.

As I got out of the tub, the water gurgling and sloshing, the drain rumbling as I released it, I thought I heard footsteps recede down the hall.

Third Encounter

It was late night. I moved slowly down the hall to my bedroom when a deep, spiced scent drifted into my lungs. I inhaled and turned, half expecting to see a person standing behind me. The air quivered as though from sudden heat. I blinked and stood very still.

The scent overpowered me. I felt dizzy and unsolid. For a moment I thought I would fall. Then a warm touch on my arm steadied me. Still, I could see nothing.

"Hello?"

Nothing.

There was a soft flutter against my lips that was just as suddenly gone. My breast was cupped in what felt like a force field of energy. The hint of a breeze (or were they invisible fingers?) stirred the hair on the back of my neck.

I thought I heard whispering and strained to listen. But the murmurings were less than a soft wind through dry leaves. Again, I could make no sense of the language.

The scent released me within moments of the encounter. I breathed in and knew he had gone.

"Why?" I asked.

Stillness answered me.

At least this time my body was left warm instead of cold. This time he'd actually touched me.

Fourth Encounter

I dreamed a man watched me though my bedroom window. The white blinds were drawn up and through the screen his face looked misty and indistinct.

He had black hair. And a long curl covered one eye and taunted his thin brown cheek.

I moved up out of my body and looked down at it and at the man who stood outside my window. My body lay, one knee bent, stomach-down. My hair fanned the pillow. My fist pressed against my chin.

The man watched me. His hair reflected night. His body was lean and tall. He was statue-still.

Traveling further upward, I broke through the roof and it parted like water. Starlight scattered across the sky like a million beacons flashing messages of loneliness. *Come to me,* they called. *Come take away the distance, the coldness, the cruelty of time.*

I flew through a wilderness of gigantic trees. Their branches and leaves rustled and hissed. They spoke but I couldn't understand them.

24

Soon he was running behind me. I heard his footsteps. I smelled his skin. My instinct was to turn and look but I didn't dare for he might catch me and my dream-self wanted to remain free.

I flitted over gulleys and ravines. The trees bent to me like tall spirits, nodding. *Run, little sister*, their whispers seemed to say. *Death is on your heels. He's right behind you. Run!*

Their hisses turned to chuckles. The wind was cold. I suddenly realized the woodland was trying to trick me. It wanted me lost so it could keep me forever. Under a tall weeping willow I stopped. "No!"

I turned.

He stood at an opening in the curtain of the tree's long hair. He was tall and slim. A blue aura outlined his form. His eyes burned with a black fire that hypnotized. Slowly his arm rose. He turned his hand up and waited.

My feet barely touched the ground as I moved toward him.

I thought I heard the willow sob.

We touched.

The coldness was like all of infinity trapped in the palm of his hand. As it burned me, I screamed.

I sat up in my bed as I jerked awake. My hand still stung where he'd clasped it.

For a long time I listened to the night.

The house was thick with quiet.

Fifth Encounter

I awoke again just before dawn.

At the foot of my bed, darker black against the shade of night, a shadow stood.

I gasped.

"Tara," whispered a voice.

I couldn't speak.

"Tara." My bed gave as though someone had just climbed upon it.

I felt him move over me and I still couldn't speak. My body was as limp as a doll's.

"I'm not a ghost," said the voice. "I won't harm you. Don't be afraid."

"I know," I replied. My voice quavered. "I'm not."

"My world is so close to yours that sometimes the shadows cross over. That's when I found you."

"Then you are a real person, just like me," I said.

"Yes."

"Can I cross into your world?"

"You have done so already without consciously knowing it," he said. "We have been drawn together. And we will continue to be."

"I felt no fear." I could finally move and I reached up to touch the silhouette of his face. The skin was smooth and firm. "It's as if I already knew."

"Understanding of this sort transcends dimensions. Time is a playground. Space is a flimsy container. We've grown beyond it." Cool fingers brushed my cheek.

"I want to be with you."

His kiss was my answer.

He enflamed my body with his hands and mouth. Over the next hour before dawn, we moved upon the bed like dancers. He pushed all the covers away from my skin. I lay naked before him. His mouth sucked on my nipples and they hardened. He parted my legs and, with my knees bent, pushed them up so that he could taste me. His tongue was like a thick, damp cloth. He lapped at my soul.

I throbbed and burned and when he entered me, his length was hard and long inside me, silken and so hot. I arched and let him suckle my breasts again.

It was like loving the dark.

His long hair tickled my chest. His penis twisted inside me.

He made me come first, something no other man had ever done to me, then with slow thrusts brought himself to the brink and stopped.

I sensed what he wanted and did not hesitate to scramble toward him. I took his length in my mouth and, using my tongue, made him harder still, and crazed. He gasped and cried out. His body swayed and arched. I could taste the salt of my love upon him and sucked harder.

He thrust into me, the tip of him cushioned against the back of my throat. My fingers caressed the testicles that dangled beneath his penis. They were taut and firm.

He smelled of sage and myrrh. I wanted to devour him.

I pulled up the organ until just the head was in my mouth. My fingers milked him and, with my lips caught against the ridge of his penis, I licked the tip with my tongue while never letting up with my lips.

When his organ jerked I pushed down on it and felt the liquid of his orgasm spurt deep in my throat. I swallowed and pulled off him, his penis still hard, still pulsing against my mouth.

His arms grabbed my shoulders before I could taste him again and, groaning, he pushed me back against the pillows. He covered me. Mingled perspiration suctioned our bodies together.

We lay together and I touched his hair, which was like silk rope, and his back which was like sun-warmed stone.

Dawn made the sky a purple wall beyond the half-open blinds of my window. In the faint light I could see his features, long-boned jaw and straight, proud nose. His eyebrows curved like the darker half of a yin and yang symbol. In the shallow hollows of his cheeks were traces of the night and a new beard. I touched the roughness there. He smiled.

"I have to go," he said softly.

"I'll go with you."

"Soon," he said. "But now it's just not possible."

"Why?"

"I can't explain."

He got up. I watched him bend to put on his pants. The muscles of his thighs and buttocks were hard beneath skin so smooth it looked freshly shaved.

"Thank you for this night," he said, stretching his arms into the sleeves of his shirt.

When I started to cry, he came close and bent over me.

"I'll still be here, Tara," he said, kissing my hair. "Always."

"I don't even know your name."

His lips curled up. The white of his teeth peeked through them. One hand reached out to my cheek and caught several tears. He held up his hand, and in the predawn glow I could see that they glistened on the tips of his fingers.

He turned and began to fade.

"What is your name?" I called out.

In a hushed tone came the answer. "I am Darkness."

As I lay in the empty room, my body still damp with love, my feelings of loneliness faded. I could hear a distant rustling, an otherworldly hum.

My house was full of whispers.

Brothers

"Love is your brother.
Love is the hero.
But first, all must travel
the dark."

"Ah, Dimitri, don't you know your pride only spurs me on? If you weren't so hard to break, so determined to give me a fight, I wouldn't bother. Now you only ask to suffer. You must want it. Somewhere in the most secret recesses of your mind, you desire this. You're begging for it even now." Baron circled him, his full pink lips lifting in a cruel smile.

Dimitri remained mute. Part of him knew it would be easier if he'd just submit. He could blank his mind, bow to this horrible man who held him against his will, and it would be over until next time. Or maybe Baron would let him go.

But another part of him denied everything that was happening. Refused to give in. If this man wanted to humiliate him, use him and rape him, then he'd have to work for it. Dimitri's pride demanded that he allow no response, that he willingly give no pleasure over to this sick individual who seemed to need his sex partners enslaved and powerless.

Forcing himself to look into his captor's eyes, Dimitri stared him down. Leather bound his wrists and ankles so he couldn't move anything but his head. He held it high. And dared the other to look away.

Baron only laughed. One hand reached out and smacked Dimitri's face. Dimitri held back his grimace and continued to stare.

"You'll learn, proud one. Oh, you'll learn," Baron promised.

Dimitri had been bar-hopping with his beautiful brother, Andreas, when Baron had grabbed him. Andreas had wanted to go to a gay bar. Since he was bisexual and dated men and women equally, he wanted to check out the 'goods'. Dimitri, who liked men too, but preferred women, agreed for just this one night. He'd do anything for his brother, whom he loved more than anyone in the world. He hadn't planned on cruising, just drinking and having a good time.

When Dimitri'd excused himself to go to the men's room, Baron was waiting for him with three burly men who escorted Dimitri at gunpoint out the back door and into a waiting van. Dimitri fought but had no chance in overcoming the four men. The last thing he remembered was being knocked on the head. He tried to fight against the blackness that followed, and failed.

When he awoke his clothes were gone. In their place were items familiar to Dimitri only from porn videos and the kinds of bizarre magazines he and his brother hated.

He wore tight leather pants which had been made without the crotch area. His back and front were exposed. On his penis had been placed a silver-studded, black leather ring. It pushed his organ out so that it jutted up as though half-hard. He felt no pleasure from it, though, only pain and anger.

In place of his shirt he wore an array of leather straps. Some of the straps had links attached and he knew they were so his captors could chain him up wherever they pleased.

On his nipples they had put clamps. The tender skin where the clamps held him was so sensitive, and the clamps were so tight, that he hardly felt them anymore. His nipples had gone numb.

His feet were bare, as were his arms. And his hands were bound securely behind his back.

He discovered, also, that he wore some sort of make up. When he'd tilted his head to brush at his shoulder with his cheek, some of the slick make up transferred to his upper arm. It had a sweet, musty odor.

Someone had tied back his dark brown, shoulder-length hair. It brushed at his spine like heavy rope.

The room he'd found himself in was cold and dark. There was no furniture, just bare walls and a bare, stained floor. He could tell by the look of one wall that it used to hold a window. Someone had plastered over it.

The only light came from a dim, naked bulb dangling from a bare wire overhead.

Upon awakening, Dimitri sat and brooded, knees drawn up to hide his naked crotch, make up smearing the leather pants where he rested his head.

Andreas, he thought. *He'll be looking for me.* Then, as a plea to all the gods, and in hopes that his brother, through the faint mental bond they'd shared as children and now, as adults, might hear him, he thought: *Please find me. Before it's too late.*

The thought of his brother warmed him. In the cool room, his body pleasantly flushed.

He knew his fate was to be raped. That thought settled upon him with an oddly detached manner. He was horrified and frightened, but it was something he could survive. He'd been fucked by men before. He hadn't liked it, but at least it wasn't as if this would be his first time.

What threw him was his costume. What frightened him more was what else these men might be up to. Sex was one part of their scheme. If he was to be tortured, too, that was something that left him cold and drained, giddy from shock.

Was he to be killed?

Would he ever be free again to see Andreas, to see his sisters, to perhaps make amends with Amanda who'd left him for another man?

Lack of answers to those questions bothered him more than the thought that someone might just be stealing him for a good time. He could handle himself well enough among bullies, and had in the past. But he had no desire to die, and he had no love for pain and the torments the body is capable of receiving.

When Baron and his men had come for him, after about a half an hour of waiting, Dimitri had kicked out at them getting in a good blow at the crotch of one of the heavies.

That was why, now, his ankles were bound.

And why, as Baron slapped him a second time for his defiant stare, he couldn't retaliate, couldn't move.

Andreas, he thought. *Where are you? Oh, dear brother, I need you now more than ever.*

"There are the rules," Baron said, as though reciting a poem. "Never look into the eyes of your master. Never disobey an order no matter how ridiculous or how trivial. Never speak unless spoken to. Never—"

Dimitri blocked him out.

He tried to continue to stare straight ahead, but his eyes were drawn by the chains and straps hanging from the ceiling. And by the swing in the corner. And to a long table where, laid out upon it like a banquet for a feast, were phallic shaped toys – some with spines all over them, some with battery packs, some with curved heads -- whips with sterling silver handles, cat-o-nine tails, lotions and drugs, harnesses and cuffs, cock-rings and wooden paddles, candles and matches.

He shivered and saw that Baron noticed.

"So, you do show a response after all. Are you frightened, proud boy? Are you thinking about what I might do to you?"

Dimitri said nothing.

"Have you ever seen a man take a fist all the way inside his ass? Perhaps I shall prepare you for just such an ordeal. Or perhaps I have more elaborate plans. Do you have a preference?"

Dimitri stared straight ahead.

"I'm speaking to you, slave!"

Dimitri tensed, waiting for the blow. When none came, his eyes moved slowly to his captor's face again.

"You'll learn," was all Baron said.

The man was really very ugly. For all his wiry little frame, he probably weighed no more than 140. In a fair fight, Dimitri at 6′2″would have been able to tackle him in seconds. Without all the help, the little man who called himself Baron would never be able to do whatever he wished with a man like Dimitri.

Baron had a sheen on the top of his head where much of his hair was missing. The hair that framed the rest of his skull was the color of antique yellow. It was frizzed and damaged on the ends. It fell to just below the tops of his ears.

His eyes were like fish eyes, pale and watery. They were too large for his narrow face which, marred by a jagged scar across one cheek, might once have been pretty. Now he was one of the homeliest men Dimitri had ever seen.

He wore much the same attire as Dimitri, only no harness or nipple clamps, and the crotch was in place on his leather trousers. His chest was flat and uninteresting. Pale curly hair covered most of it and his belly.

Dimitri shuddered inwardly to think this man would soon be pressed against him, ready to have his way with him.

You're an ugly little demon, he thought. Aloud, he said nothing.

"Let's see," Baron said, circling him again. "Yes, you'll do nicely for what I have in mind. Very nicely indeed." Dimitri felt a hand on his buttock and every muscle tensed, every part of him screamed in denial.

The hand patted him. "Yes," Baron droned, "very nice indeed. You must work out often. You must jog. Do you jog? It's bad for the joints, you know."

Dimitri's teeth hurt from gritting them so hard.

Now in front, Baron's hand touched his cock. Dimitri closed his eyes. His face heated but he held his breath and made no other response.

"This is quite large. I might like to suck on it. Would you like that? I might even let you come, if you're a good boy."

The hand stroked him, rough palm, rough grip. His balls were fondled, then suddenly jerked. The pain flashed through his head but still he kept quiet.

Andreas, please come, he thought through the sudden sting in his eyes.

"Very nice, pretty, even. And circumcised. But aren't you Greek? I didn't think Greek men had that done. I didn't think that at all. I myself prefer circumcised cocks, though. This is your lucky day."

The hand batted at him and because of the leather cock ring, his penis bobbed gently. With pride, Dimitr noted that he did not respond in the least. This man disgusted him. He wouldn't give him the pleasure of showing a response even if the man was the best cocksucker in the world. It was his goal, his mission to remain impotent until he was rescued, or until he died. His determination gave him strength. His will was strong.

Baron moved away and Dimitri opened his eyes.

"Rod. Alexander. Come!"

Two of the men who'd muscled him from the gay bar's bathroom entered. They came to a stop, one on either side of Baron.

"Prepare his mouth," Baron ordered.

One went to the table. Dimitri turned to watch him but was slapped by Baron again. "On your knees."

Dimitri stood.

"I said, on your knees! Rod, show him."

Rod came behind him and placed his hands on his shoulders, roughly pushing. Then he kicked at the insides of Dimitri's knees and they buckled. Dimitri fell, his vision sparking at the jarring pain of his kneecaps hitting the hard floor.

Alexander returned from the table with a bottle of some kind of pink gel in his hand. He opened the lid and held it out to Baron who took it absently.

"I want to see how well he sucks cock. I want to watch him do both of you," Baron said.

Dimitri gritted his teeth harder as Rod and Alexander undid their leather crotches. Two flaccid cocks were exposed.

34

Rod's was thick, Alexander's was long. Alexander's balls were huge. He was the first to thrust himself into Dimitri's face. The pointed head pushed against his tightly closed lips.

"If you bite him," Baron warned, "I'll bite you. Everything you do to them will be, in turn, done to you. If you're good, you get it good."

Alexander pushed again at Dimitri's mouth. Dimitri closed his eyes and didn't move. Alexander continued to push.

A sharp crack split the air and Dimitri jumped. His flank stung where a whip had hit him.

"Open your mouth, slave!" Baron ordered.

Dimitri turned away. The whip cracked again.

As he gasped, Alexander's long cock pushed into his mouth. He gagged as the man thrust back and forth. "Not very good, master," Alexander reported. "Too much teeth."

The whip stung him a third time on the left buttock. He felt the hand touch the crack of his ass and part it. "Suck him," came the command.

Dimitri eased up on the long cock and softly sucked. "Better," Alexander said.

"Good. Coat yourself and see how he likes that," Baron ordered.

Dimitri opened his eyes. What was this?

Alexander took a handful of gel from Baron and spread it over his penis. Rod was doing the same. "You'll like it," Baron said. "It tastes pretty good and it'll help them keep their hard-ons for a long time so you'll have to suck them hard. Could take hours. You'd better do a good job."

Now he understood. It was a desensitizing lotion. Their sensations would be minimized and they wouldn't come prematurely.

Alexander forced his cock into his mouth again. Already it had grown about two inches. It was clear Alexander liked what Dimitri was doing.

Rod stepped forward and petted Dimitri's tied back hair. "He's a pretty one, isn't he?"

"Yes," Baron answered. "A prime catch."

They all laughed.

Of all the men, Dimitri thought Alexander was the best looking. He had blond, curly hair and a good tan. His body was hard and muscular. Rod's hair was nearly shaved off. And his muscles, though large, were pale. And he was too short, his face too square for Dimitri's tastes. His cock was short and thick, and very red. Rather ugly. Alexander's was golden. Even pretty. But Dimitri allowed the thought to go no further.

Rod shoved his cock into Dimitri's mouth as Alexander pulled out. Dimitri thought for a moment that he would vomit. The urge passed and he closed his eyes pretending he was anywhere else—with his brother, with Amanda—and licked and sucked.

The gel both men used tasted of cinnamon. Dimitri had, up until today, liked cinnamon. Now he'd never be able to eat it again.

Both men shoved into his mouth for what seemed to Dimitri like hours while Baron watched and directed. He made them change positions occasionally. First he made Rod and Alexander lie down on the cold floor, facing each other, their legs overlapping so that their balls pressed together. Dimitri had to bend over them and suck one while milking the other. Then Baron ordered him to suck them both in together. The two cocks stretched his mouth painfully.

Next Baron told Dimitri to lie down. The cold floor against his exposed, whipped buttocks stung. Taking turns, Rod and Alexander squatted over him and thrust deeply into his mouth. Dimitri hated every moment of it.

At long last, Rod came, squirting into Dimitri's mouth, making him wretch and gag.

Soon after, Alexander came all over his chest.

"Very good," Baron said.

Dimitri didn't look at him. Instead, he stared straight up at the ceiling, trying to ignore the harnesses that hung there.

"It was great," Rod said.

"Yeah," Alexander agreed.

"Maybe he'll get a little in return, then," Baron said.

"His cock is beautiful. I'd love a taste," Alexander said.

"Go ahead—"

Dimitri tensed again, his heart beating rapidly. Then he closed his eyes and tried to ignore the sensations. Alexander's hot mouth engulfed him all the way to the ring. Dimitri had no trouble not responding. All he had to do was think of Baron's ugly face and his body was frozen from any response. He held his knees together and that helped, too.

After awhile, Alexander stopped mouthing him. "Guess he doesn't like it," he said softly.

"Next, we shave him. I want his chest shaved. His balls shaved. His legs shaved. And his ass shaved. Let him kept the rest."

The two strong men lifted Dimitri onto a table next to a bucket of water and some disposable razors.

Carefully, they shaved him. When they started to shave his testicles, Dimitri cried out and shoved them away. His punishment was a whipping that stung but did not draw blood. When they tried to shave his balls a second time, strong hands spreading his legs at the knees while his feet remained bound, he squirmed.

"Cut him if he moves again," Baron ordered.

Dimitri shivered and lay still.

They did a good job. He was not cut once and the warm water against his groin felt relaxing as they rinsed him. Then they gently turned him over and did the same thing to his ass. With his face pressed tightly to the tabletop, his body shaking, tears formed and fell. Luckily no one saw and he was saved from further humiliation.

After he was rinsed again, Baron ordered his ass prepared. Alexander and Rod covered his backside with lotions and gels. They probed him with gel-covered fingers, and pushed generous amounts inside him.

That was when Dimitri realized they had no intention of hurting him. The care with which they took to shave him, to whip him without drawing blood, to lubricate him for intercourse, proved that. A part of him was relieved. Another part of him continued to be outraged.

After he was prepared, Baron ordered him to be attached to a contraption that hung from the ceiling. Dimitri's ankles were unbound and the ankle cuffs were attached to two separate chains. The harness he wore snapped onto more cables and chains. Baron pulled at some lines at the end of the room and Dimitri was raised a few feet from the floor, his legs spread and sticking up in the air, his head back, nearly upside down. His cock hung toward his belly now. His legs and ass were spread wide open. He grimaced and the tears returned. Shutting his eyes tightly, he waited.

Baron approached. He could hear the booted footsteps as the man walked around him. "Very nice. Very nice. You are perfect now. Ready for me."

Dimitri stole a peek at the room from his upside down position. Rod and Alexander stood back, watching. Baron was not in view, but he could tell from the bootsteps, and the ugly little man's heavy breathing, that he stood behind him, close to his exposed genitals and rump.

"A little lower, please," Baron ordered.

He opened his eyes a crack and saw Alexander approach the ropes at the wall. He adjusted one. Dimitri's legs dropped a few inches. His ass lowered.

"Perfect," Baron said.

He heard the rip of a zipper coming open. He heard the man's sick sigh. Then he felt the tip of a small penis spread his ass. He almost laughed at the irony. *All this and I'm going to be raped by a little man with four inches!*

But he still hated it when the small cock entered him. He hated the way the man grunted when his pelvis hit his buttocks. He hated the way the sharp fingers poked at his thighs where Baron held him in place. H e hated the feel of swaying, of not having any friction on his body but that little cock inside him and the little hands on his thighs.

Oh, Andreas, he thought. *Where are you?*

"Rod," Baron said, between grunts and thrusts. "If you want him to suck you again, be my guest."

Rod stepped forward to where Dimitri's head still hung upside down. He held his thick cock and steered it toward Dimitri's face. He put it in his mouth as Baron thrust forward with all his might. Then they got a rhythm going. Baron would push Dimitri onto Rod's cock, then as Baron pulled out, Rod pushed in. They swung him back and forth between them.

Baron thrust for many minutes before Rod came. He came fast and hard. Baron laughed and said, "Good boy. Good boy," as Rod's sperm dripped down Dimitri's face.

"Now suck him off, Rod-man."

"I'll try."

Dimitri closed his eyes as the shaved head and pale mouth descended on his own organ which hung down over his belly. Rod licked underneath it, swirled the balls in his mouth, and deep-throated. Dimitri thought that at another time it might be good, even great, but now he refused to give in. He felt a heat begin to build and clamped firmly down on it. "Woah. Do that again, boy!"

Rod held him between two fingers and continued to suck. Dimitri concentrated on not feeling. But the man was damn good! It was so hard to resist. His muscles contracted again.

"Ahh," Baron said and Dimitri felt him come.

Even after Baron pulled out, Rod continued to suck him. Baron came over to watch. "Any progress?" he asked.

Rod pulled off and looked at the wet organ which continued to flop against Dimitri's belly. "Don't look like it."

"He's a stubborn one," Baron said. "But we'll get him to come yet. It is, after all, only fair."

They tried everything. Dildos up his slick ass. Cream to heighten sensation. More cock rings to make him hard.

They only succeeded in making Dimitri more angry, more determined than ever not to show any response.

As they were forcing him to fellate Alexander a second time, a large crack sounded from one side of the room. Alexander gave a yelp and pulled out of Dimitri's mouth at once. Baron and Rod froze.

"What the fuck?" Baron yelled.

"Get away from him! Now! Or I'll blow your head off!"

The voice was familiar to Dimitri, but he wasn't sure. Could it be true? Were his thoughts received? "Andreas," he called. His voice was so hoarse it came out a whisper.

"Get away from him!" Andreas yelled again.

Baron, Rod and Alexander all filed to one corner of the room. Dimitri heard footsteps, saw the shadows of many men. It was obvious Andreas had been smart enough to come armed and with back up.

The tears started. Dimitri grimaced.

Andreas handed the gun off to another man and came up alongside Dimitri. "Looks like you're having a bad day," he said softly. Then he looked up. "Sandy, get him down."

Sandy, whoever that was, must have known what to do, for he was instantly lowered, his brother's arms around him, cushioning him from the cold, hard floor.

"You okay?" Andreas asked.

Dimitri couldn't see for his tears. He gasped. "I don't know." He wanted to hug him, but his hands were still bound together. Instead, he pressed his head against the warm, safe chest.

Andreas reached down and pulled the dildo from his ass. It felt so good.

"Bastards," Andreas muttered under his breath. "I know you hate that most."

Next he undid the cock ring. Dimitri felt instantly released, and his cock sprang up at the sudden sensation of

40

freedom, of release. Andreas' hands were so gentle, and Dimitri was so overstimulated, that he instantly hardened. He thrust against his brother's hand, groaning. Andreas. Childhood playmate. Blond to his brunet. Womb twin and first born. They'd done everything together from the moment they breathed life. Andreas, his hero. His beautiful brother.

"Shhh," Andreas said. "You'll be okay. I heard you call me, you know." He stroked him gently from flared tip to base.

"Oh god," Dimitri whispered, pressing against the only man he'd ever truly loved, and the semen shot from him like fire.

Season of Water and Flame

"In the yellowing autumn grasses
parched for rain
I lie in wait
for spring."

Though it rained earlier in the day, the sun is fierce. The sky is like a roiling swamp. Copper/green. Splotched gray. With currents of air that are liquid to the touch.

I go to the gate. The wind is blue-hot. The damp grass is yellow, still withered from the heat.

The gate drips with rainwater, the polished wood dark under my pale hand. It swings open without a sound.

I look into my neighbor's hidden yard.

It contains shades of yellow unimaginable. Puce. Ochre. Sienna. Gold. Even the scents in his yard are yellow: lemon, autumn, flame.

A tree on a dying grass-covered hill bows its tawny leaves, some already spotting the ground. The garden is full of buttery clay dirt. And the patio door and the back of the house are both painted an ivory yellow that is sometimes called buff, sometimes cream.

The only break in the monotony of shades is an island of brilliant blue, purer than the sky, bright as a mirror. In the middle of the yard it sits, surrounded by sand-colored concrete. The swimming pool.

My hair is hot against the back of my neck. My swimsuit straps clutch at my shoulders. The pool is my destination, a process of obvious natural selection in this hundred degree heat.

I'm grateful for my neighbor's open invitation to use his pool at any time. It waits, still waters like a vast diamond waiting to be probed.

I fold my towel and leave it on a chair by the pool-edge.

Already my skin cools, predicting the envelope of water, the soothing gush, the momentary escape from this world into one of lethargic silence.

My toes curl over the edge of concrete, pressing tightly, tensing along with the rest of my arched body for the dive.

I jump.

My arms and head submerge first, the water like a million soft hands, like an early spring breeze after a thaw.

Bubbles blow out of my nose and mouth. I can barely taste the sharp chlorine. This world is a soft-focused vision of light.

Underwater, I swim the entire length of the pool. As I surface, the two worlds, water and air, merge and for a single moment I imagine I am in neither place but in between, encased in a bubble outside time. I can see a hundred doorways, large and small, and a hundred different types of light. The universe not only curves around my bubble, but shoots through these doorways breathing into unseen dimensions and alien night.

As I break the liquid ceiling, my lungs heave. The humid air burns. Waves lap at the pool-sides with quiet licking sounds. My feet find the bottom as my palms push my hair away from my face. I blink.

The world is yellow again, and old.

Automatically, my body seeks the security of cool submerging. I propel myself forward, kicking, and begin a series of lazy laps.

Water splashes all around me. Damp clumps of my hair float around me like a dark cloud. My mind forgets there are such things as unhappiness, ugliness, injustice. I am in a perfect world where everything washes upon everything else and is joined together in blazing clarity.

As my body tires, I make for the shallow end. Back resting against the side, elbows propped on the edge, I push through the heaving liquid with my legs. The water is almost a live thing, and I its lover to devour. I take deep breaths of warm air and close my eyes.

A thump to my right startles me out of my doze.

He stands by the patio door, towel in hand, black swim trunks clinging to his narrow, lean hips.

My chest tightens. I didn't think he was home.

Like a cat, he moves silently forward. His straight black hair catches gold from the land, blue from the pool. He is far older than I, about 45 to my mere 20, so my obsession with him, my feelings of unease and insecurity when I am around him, make no sense. As a rule, I am not attracted to older men. But this one compels. His dark eyes are like jewels lit with a light from deep places. His olive skin, long fingers and aristocratic nose draw him in and charm me.

But he hasn't a clue as to my true feelings.

I'm just a kooky kid, a stray neighbor with nothing else to do than spy on him from my second story window as he comes and goes from various motion picture studios where he directs films for a living.

He says nothing as he approaches the pool. His dive is clean and powerful. His streamlined body enters the water in a neat impact that creates only minor wakes.

As he begins his laps, I watch. He is a dark line shooting through pale fluid, his strokes mechanically strong. I count as he swims. He does 40 lengths before slowing.

What I know about this man is mostly what I've read. Even living right next door to him offers few clues. I know he was married once, and that his wife died of a strange disease. I know he has two grown children, one married, one not. He lives alone and has few visitors. I've seen his granddaughter (she must be a granddaughter) playing in the backyard on two occasions. The tabloids say her name is Brooke, and she is four years old.

I've been inside his house only once, and that's because I went there to invite him to a party. (Of course he didn't come.) He keeps the shades drawn and everything is very dark. The

44

couch is pine green, the velvet curtains a rich jade. The floors are dark wood, as are the award-laden bookcases that line the walls. When I was there, everything looked covered in a thin sheen of dust. What light leaked around the heavy drapes illumined the dust and filled the room with subtle rainbows.

Now he swims slowly toward me where I crouch in the shallows. My skin tingles. I cannot meet his eyes.

"Hello," he says, drawing up his knees and treading water. His hair is a black helmet melted on his head. His lashes flash with chlorine tears.

"Hi." I squint at him and smile. "I didn't think you were home."

He ignores the comment. "This day is like fire," he says. "I'm glad to see you're making use of the pool."

"I suppose I should have asked you first," I say.

"I told you you were welcome to use it any time." His voice is rough and low. "I meant it."

"Thanks."

His full lips curve.

"You swim well," I comment.

He lets his feet down and stands. The water rushes off him in glistening rivulets. "It's good exercise. I haven't been able to do it in awhile. The strange weather, you know."

I nod. One day cold, the next hot. The world is changing faster than people can see. "Are you tired?" I ask. After all those laps, his breathing is calm and even.

He smiles and the even white teeth lighten his composure. "No. Are you?"

"No, but I really should be going. My fingers are starting to wrinkle."

"But it's so hot," he says quietly. "I've never know it to be so hot." He looks up, almost sadly, to the boiling copper sky. "What's happening to our planet?"

"Disrespect," I say.

When he looks back at me his eyes are as dark as the lives of lonely children, as the shadows he keeps locked inside his house. My chest aches. "I will never understand," he says.

He lives in a world of unreality. It's sad when people don't notice, until it's too late, when things change and die. "I wanted a garden," he almost whispers. "Now nothing will grow."

"Maybe in the spring," I say hopefully.

"Maybe."

I don't look away from him now as his eyes search my face. Darkness. Desolation. Oblivion. Of its own accord, my hand reaches out.

"Dina." My hand stops. "How old are you?"

"Twenty."

"It's not fair."

"What?"

"What my generation has done to yours."

I bow my head. "I don't blame you."

After a moment, he says, "I've seen you."

"Seen me?"

"Watching me." He gestures toward my house beyond his four foot wooden fence. "From your upstairs window. What do you see, Dina? What are you thinking?"

"I...I don't know."

"You're a writer?"

I nod.

"Do you write about me? Do you dream things could be different?"

"I...I guess." He has been so aloof always. I never thought to be confronted like this. I haven't any prepared answers.

"I don't see many people. By choice. Some call me bitter." He laughs without smiling. "I just don't like people. Strange in my line of work, isn't it?"

"Yeah."

"But you, you're different. You looked sixteen when you came over that night to invite me to your party. But you're really twenty. Well, I was fooled. You have young eyes."

"You have the eyes of purgatory," I blurt.

His brow rises. "How observant. And how sensitive of you to notice."

"I notice unhappy people," I say. "I can't help it. They draw me to them."

"I have few friends," he says.

"I know."

He turns his head. The sky reflected in his hair is chipped and alive. "Could you really want someone like me?"

I feel my lips part, my law slacken in amazed shock. I can't answer. I can't breathe.

"This planet is dying. Through ignorance, I've helped to kill it. Do you still want me?"

Warm tears mist my eyes.

"I'm forty-five. There are wrinkles around my mouth and eyes. Do you still want me?"

My body trembles.

"I live in the dark most of the time. I'm a terrible housekeeper. And all I wanted was a garden." His voice breaks. "Now you know who I am. Who are you that you could want me? Who are you?"

My voice sounds small and shrill. "Just Dina," I answer. "I live next door."

The water swirls around his waist as he wades toward me. When his hand touches my shoulder it is hotter than the air, than the day that brought me here.

"Dina." His voice is like a quiet hum. He bends down and kisses me lightly on the forehead. "Damn you for making me feel this right now. I closed myself off years ago. I wanted it that way. Now you've come. Damn you."

But he doesn't mean it. I can tell he doesn't mean what he says. I stare up at him, slowly coming to life all over my body. "But I do want you."

"You say that because you don't know any better. But you can't help it that you're so naïve." Then he takes me in his arms and presses his lips to mine.

My body floats to meet his. My mouth opens.

There is a sound like wings fluttering on water. My breath is like a stone in my lungs. My legs brush against his in the suddenly thick fluid of the pool. The effect electrifies me and the feeling of that, while floating in water, is extremely intense.

His hands are in my tangles of damp hair. Mine clutch at his shoulders. He moves against me like a fish, his body and mine floating together, apart, then back together.

He guides me to the steps where the water is two feet at the lowest step, and at the top step only inches deep. He pushes me against them and presses himself to me.

Now his hands are on my shoulders sweeping my swimsuit straps down. When the water swirls against my breasts they grow harder. His hand follows the water-path, his fingers mold and squeeze.

I gasp for air as he kisses my throat. His hands push my suit to my hips and caress my waist. The softness and pressure of him and the pool creates a quick heat between my legs.

I have to touch. I can't hold back. My hands move up and down his back. They push at his waistband and delve beneath to the firm roundness which I stroke and squeeze.

He does the same to me, pushing the elastic material past my hips, down my thighs and, finally, off as I step away and let the thin one-piece float free.

The water explores every crevice of my body. His hands follow.

Soon I have his trunks off him and our bodies, with only eddies of water between us, meet and brush together. His penis floats against the thatch of hair just below my abdomen. It's hard and warm. My hand moves to touch it.

He is sucking at my half-submerged breast as he enters me. One swift stroke and I'm impaled. My body is liquid as the pool. Where he probes and thrusts, I am fevered and slick. I lean against the concrete steps for support and push up onto him. His eyes close in pleasure.

My hands on his hips, I pull him to me. I can't get enough. I want more.

He thrusts harder. The heat between us increases.

I look up at the boiling sky as water laps between my breasts, as his tongue laps, his cheek caresses, and think: *You may be dying, but I'm alive! Alive!*

I have disturbed his dust. I have awakened the beast. I have taken the dark and twisted it until it is inside my light and can never escape.

His hand touches that most secret of spots just above where he enters me. His finger rubs, teases.

I can't see the yellow world anymore, only my thoughts filled with blue and green, only his diamond pool and the water gliding as he moves inside me.

My muscles throb. The spirit of my skin feels like it is being lifted from me, so beautiful, so ecstatic. He kisses my mouth as an exclamation of surprise bursts forth. My orgasm lasts until I feel him allow all restraints to go, until he bursts inside me like a nova, the warmth of his seed mingling with the heat of my own cushioning response.

His palms press my breasts, my waist, my back. He pets me and murmurs, "What you do to me, what you do."

My wet hair clings to my shoulders. The water is the embrace of aphrodisiac nectar.

Even after he's through, he doesn't pull out. Instead, he continues to gently thrust, keeping us merged, clinging to this freshness of life.

For both of us this new world is a better place.

We are on the inside of a different reality, looking out at a water-blue sky.

Boys

*"Friends form thoughts within
each other's minds
and touch those places
of secrets and shadows
known only to the
ghost of love."*

Jesse hopped up the porch steps two at a time and rapped loudly on the old screen door. The summer grass had browned and now a dry wind blew scents of over-ripened weeds and hay through the streets. Everything seemed dry. Even the pale sky.

"Who is it?" called a woman's voice.

"Jesse." His voice cracked. "Is Zach home?"

"In his room. You can go on up. And you boys don't disturb me now, you hear? No noise. I'm watching a good movie that starts in five minutes and I don't want to be interrupted."

The screen door clacked shut behind him. "Okay, Mrs. McCoy. Thanks."

He bounded up the carpeted stairs, his oversized tennis shoes thumping like thunder.

Zach's door was open. "Hey," Jesse said.

"Come in." He rolled over on the bed and put down the magazine he'd been reading. "Close the door."

Jesse obeyed and turned to face him. "Your mom's watching a movie. She doesn't want to be disturbed."

"Perfect," Zach said. "Come here."

Jesse approached. Though he was just fifteen, he wasn't so young and naïve as to be unaware of the magazine Zach was reading. On the cover were the words, *HARD INCHES.* Inside were pictures of naked men.

50

"Look at this guy," Zach said. "Man, that must be fake."

Jesse followed his gaze as Zach opened the magazine to a color foldout. His body felt strange as he looked at the hard organ that jutted between the muscle-man's legs. He himself was of average size. He wondered if that was all right.

"I don't get why you look at these magazines all the time," Jesse said.

"Don't you like 'em?" Zach asked.

"Well, yeah. But I like Playboy, too."

"Sure, but it'll only frustrate you. Girls aren't even willing. But boys are."

"How do you know?"

"Oh," he said cryptically, which Jesse hated, "I just do."

"How?" he asked again.

"Promise you won't tell?"

"I'll make a pact with you. If I tell, the next time I come to your house I'll bring you fifty bucks."

"Okay." Zach smiled. His full lips and straight white teeth made Jesse envious. His own mouth was small and firm. His face was slightly pointed. His hair, a dull brown cap of perfectly straight locks was nothing compared to Zach's thick dark curls. And Zach's skin was a shade darker than bronze and looked so smooth.

"Okay," Jesse prompted. "Talk."

"You know Gene the Machine?"

"The football player?" His insides fell.

"Well, he has gym the same time I do. I saw him after class in one of the shower stalls. He and Dirk the jerk. You know. Dirk was sucking him off. I couldn't even believe it. Made me hard just watching."

"No way," Jesse breathed.

"It's true. And he dates Suzy Smoochie so it's gotta be okay. He just gets it where he can. Suzy's probably on the rag or doesn't put out or something."

"Shit." Jesse knelt, feeling suddenly weak-kneed, by the side of the bed.

"Yeah. Shit."

"So," Jesse said slowly. "What'd he look like?"

Zach hit him on the shoulder and snickered. "You try so hard to pretend you're not interested, then you ask that? Hell, Jesse, you need these magazines more than I do."

"So, tell me. I made the pact with you. Come on."

"Well, he was huge."

"Huge?"

"Yep. And he was real dark red, real thick. Dirk took him all the way in, you know. It's called deep-throating."

"I know," Jesse said, rolling his eyes.

"Gene was really getting' off. His head was back and he was moaning. I was afraid the coach would hear. But no one came. They didn't know I was there, either."

"Did you stick around?" Jesse asked. "Did you watch it all?"

"You mean did I see him come?"

Jesse nodded, looking down.

"Yeah. Dirk-i-poo swallowed most of it. The homo."

"Don't say that," Jesse said.

"What?"

"Don't say 'homo' like that. I mean, you look at this stuff. You don't think it's really wrong, do you?"

Well, if you have to hide it from your parents, it's probably wrong," Zach said, giggling.

"No, I mean that it's not really crazy or something. You aren't going to end up in the bin for it, are you?"

"Hell, no. Don't be so paranoid." Zach hit his shoulder again. "So, you want to look at more of my magazines?"

Jesse shrugged.

"I've got a real special one."

"What?"

"Men doing it. Together."

"No way!"

"It's right here," he said, leaning down and digging under his bed. He handed it to Jesse. On the cover was a man with

52

short dark hair sucking off a blond guy with an enormous cock.

"Ohmigod," Jesse said, just staring.

"Take a look."

Slowly, Jesse turned the pages. Picture after picture showed men in varying sexual positions. "I can't believe they really do that," Jesse said.

"What are you, naïve?"

He shook his head.

"Don't tell me you never thought about sticking it up some guy's ass. You know, just for fun."

"Well, I never thought about it, not really."

Zach grinned. "I have. But I don't know if I'd like it done to me. God, those guys are big."

"Yeah." Jesse's heart was beating faster. His penis was hard beneath his jeans. His balls ached.

"Know what?"

Jesse looked up. "What?"

"I'm horny as hell now looking at these."

Jesse laughed, relieved he wasn't alone. "Me, too."

"Just for an experiment now, and don't laugh, we could, well, uh, you know, suck a little on each other. It would feel good and then we wouldn't have to sit here all uncomfortable."

Jesse's face heated. He thought that Zach could surely feel his heat. "I don't know."'

"Why not? What could happen? You shy or what?"

"Kinda."

"I'll bet you've never done it. Not even with a girl."

"Well…"

Zach laughed.

Jesse frowned. "Hey. Don't laugh at me."

Zach stopped and looked at him seriously. "Okay. I'm sorry. I'm just nervous. About asking you and all. I know you're shy. But I wouldn't tell no one. And I'd be real good, you know, gentle and all."

Jesse took a deep breath. "Okay, what do we do?"

"Lock the door first."

Jesse got up and flipped the lock from the inside.

"Okay," Zach said, "come up here on the bed."

Jesse did as he was told and sat beside him. "Now at the same time, we both take off our pants, underwear and all, okay?"

Jesse smiled and ducked his head. "Okay."

"One, two, three."

They busied themselves undoing buttons and snaps. Zach's were on the floor in a heap as Jesse was still pulling his down. Jesse turned. Zach was staring at him. He blushed, seeing that his thin penis was hard as a rock and flushed.

His eyes moved to Zach's. It was bigger than Jesse's, but not by much. It was dark olive, almost green, and jutted from a thatch of black shiny curls.

"I think if you touch me, I'll come real fast," Zach said.

"Me, too," Jesse echoed.

"Well then we'll just have to do it again, make it last longer the second time. For now it's just release. After, we'll experiment."

"Experiment?"

"Yeah. With different positions and stuff. Like in the pictures. But none of that ass-fucking stuff."

"Yeah," said Jesse. "None of that ass-fucking stuff."

"Want me to go first?" Zach asked.

Jesse nodded.

"Then lie back."

Hesitantly, Jesse scooted up in the bed and lay on Zach's *Star Wars* pillowcase. His penis bobbed as he moved. Zach knelt between his legs and touched the tip with his tongue. Jesse watched, fascinated. Electrical charges ran from his cock to his balls and throughout his body.

Zach's whole, hot mouth dropped over his erection and encased it. Jesse forgot how to breathe. The wet mouth descended, then as it pulled up the pressure increased. Zach came off it with a pop. "Okay?"

Jesse finally breathed out. "More than okay," he said breathily.

Zach smiled. "You taste good."

Jesse watched as his friend went down on him again, his fingers encircling his penis at the base, then moving lower to tickle his balls. He thrust up without warning. He didn't mean to but he couldn't help it. Zach took it all in stride and gripped Jesse's hips with both hands.

"Jesus, Zach!" Jesse burst out. Then he let out a cry and came hard, deep in Zach's liquid mouth.

His penis throbbed and jerked, the liquid shooting through it burning his organ with jets of pleasure.

Zach drank it all, which Jesse hadn't expected him to do. Would Zach want him to drink his semen as well?

When Jesse was finished, Zach moved off him. His penis was still rock hard, still flushed, but the urgency was gone for the moment. His mind reeled. It had felt so good.

"My turn," Zach said, plopping beside Jesse onto his back.

Jesse sat up. He stared at Zach's erection for a moment, his heart thumping madly. Then he moved and knelt, the way Zach had, between his friend's bent, spread legs.

First he touched Zach with an open palm. The penis bobbed in reaction. Zach groaned. "Hurry, Jesse."

Jesse bent down, his palm pressed against Zach's balls, the cock pointing straight up. He opened his mouth and let the penis slide in. It was remarkably warm and smooth, and tasted slightly of salt and soap. He licked the underside with his tongue, sucked slightly with his lips careful not to press too hard with his teeth. He'd heard horror stories from guys who went out with girls who bit them. Now he only wanted to give pleasure to Zach.

Zach was tossing his head, moaning. Jesse pushed himself down as far as he could on the hard organ, then pulled up.

When the head left his mouth, he made a sucking sound that filled him with pleasure and made his own balls ache again.

Zach grabbed his head and pushed at him. "Do it fast. Do it hard," he ordered.

Jesse complied. He pushed his saliva forward in his mouth, then went down on Zach again, quickly, then back up. The rhythm seemed natural enough and he speeded it up.

After about five times, Zach's penis spasmed. He could feel it jerk against his tongue. Then a stream of hot liquid squirted in his mouth. He swallowed automatically.

"Oh Jesse," Zach called, still coming. "Oh yeah."

Afterwards, they lay side by side on the bed, naked from the waists down. "Now what should we do?" Jesse asked.

"Look at more magazines. I like to stroke myself while I look at 'em. Here." He handed Jesse one and grabbed one for himself. Apparently he had stacks of them under his bed.

Jesse looked at the picture of two men end to end, one straddling the other, one on his back, and elbowed Zach. "We oughta try this one next," he suggested.

"Sure. Whatever you want. Damn you're mouth is hot." He grinned. "My balls are still aching."

"Mine, too," Jesse agreed.

For awhile they looked at pictures and stroked themselves. Then Zach turned. "I'm ready for you again," he said.

Jesse could only nod. His own penis was hard as a rock.

"Let's try the position in that picture."

"Okay."

Zach turned in the bed until his head was at Jesse's cock, and his cock found Jesse. Then he straddled Jesse's head and went down on his erect penis at the same time. Jesse gasped and when his mouth opened Zach shoved himself in and thrust.

Zach lifted up. "Oh that feels good."

Jesse could only grunt as he sucked the cock that came from above him and moved as if of its own accord, in and out of his mouth.

Zach's wet mouth was so hot on his burning skin that he couldn't help but thrust upwards a few times.

Jesse felt Zach's hands on his thighs, pushing him, spreading them. Then he felt Zach's mouth move lower and encase his balls. Zach licked them and sucked them, then moved back up. Jesse groaned as he sucked on Zach. Soon both were grunting and moaning.

Jesse pushed up just as Zach went down all the way on him and his cock burst inside that tight wetness. His body shook. He felt crazy and sucked on Zach harder. Zach pushed in and out, fast and hard and jerked, liquid filling Jesse's mouth with tangy heat and musk.

Zach collapsed on top of Jesse. For a minute, neither boy moved. Finally Zach rolled off. His eyes were closed, his mouth curved up. "I could do that with you all day."

"Shit," Jesse said.

They giggled.

The afternoon light played rainbows in Zach's curly black hair. His dark eyes looked haunted and very, very bright.

"You're so good," Zach whispered, close to Jesse's ear.

"You, too. I didn't know it could be like this."

They embraced and clung to each other in the small, twin bed. Their half hard penises pressed against each other. Their thin bodies, one light, one dark, were like a narrow yin and yang symbol.

"You know," Jesse said, "I'd do anything for you."

"Me, too," Zach said.

"I think I do want to borrow some of your magazines."

"Any time."

Jesse stared at the face so close to his. The dark eyes looked fathomless, beautiful. His heart swelled and, again, his penis.

I love you, he thought.

Aloud, he said, "You're my best friend, you know."

"I know," Zach replied. He smiled. Jesse squeezed him tighter and very lightly, very quickly, he kissed Zach on the lips.

Quietly Purple

"Outside my window
dusk drifts into night.
I am liquid with longing
as the sky grows
quietly purple."

Dorian Mayer finished writing his name on the front chalkboard and turned.

"My name is Mr. Mayer," he said, smiling. "And I'll be your teacher for the duration of this class which is, I believe, ten weeks."

The new students, mostly girls, who had shown up for his elective creative writing class, stared at him with eager, upturned faces. Most were between sixteen and eighteen years of age. This was a class offered only to advanced and gifted students and was worth two college credits.

Dorian smiled as he surveyed these prospective writers. There were fifteen in all, he noted, and they came in all shapes and sizes, and all shades from ivory to brown. One dark-haired girl with pale, almond-shaped eyes smiled as their gazes met. He smiled back and thought: *She's beautiful.* He went on to look at each student in turn. Though they were all uniquely beautiful in their own way, the first made an impression. The rest of the students made little impact on him. He turned back to the dark one with pale eyes who sat to the side and halfway back in the room.

"Starting with you," he said, gesturing toward her, "we'll first get to know each other by introducing ourselves, name, age and why you took this class."

"Jade Simmons," she said quietly. "I'm sixteen. I like writing poetry mostly. The class sounded interesting. I've written one story."

"Oh?" Dorian asked. "What about?"

"Uh," she hesitated, blushing fiercely. Dorian smiled to put her at ease. "It was about sex."

Suddenly he didn't know if he was standing in the classroom or falling into a deep chasm. He cleared his throat among the snickers of the rest of the class.

It only took him seconds to right himself, and he showed no outward response of shock to her bold answer. Amid the waves of giggles that filled the classroom air, he said, "That's very good. Writing about our feelings, both physical and mental, is how we get started." He turned, frowning at the rest of the class. "By the way, if you think you can shock me, you're most likely mistaken. I'm a voracious reader. Whatever you write, I've probably read the subject before. Your job is to tell it in a new and unique fashion, with an inner natural language which I hope this class will help you to discover." He turned back to the girl. "Thank you for your honesty, Jade." His pulse was racing. How had she made such an impact on him in such a short span of time? Class was only five minutes old!

He glanced at the young man behind Jade. "And you?"

The first half of class time was spent finishing the introductions. During the second half, Dorian talked about writing techniques while concentrating on deliberately avoiding the girl, Jade's, rapt gaze.

But even out the corner of his eye, he couldn't help but notice how soft and satiny her dark hair looked, how it reflected all light and became multi-colored, how her pale eyes flashed like two little beacons in her face.

She was bewitching.

His body made it obvious to his mind that he wanted her.

But she was one of the youngest, sixteen. As far as Dorian was concerned, body and soul, she was off-limits. There was no question about it. No question at all.

He gave them their first assignment just before the bell rang to excuse them. They were to write a poem or short story.

60

As the class filed out, he turned his back on them to erase the board. His arm moved in slow, deliberate circles. He inhaled the chalk scent, breathed out slowly.

"Mr. Mayer?"

He turned at the sound of the voice. "Yes?" As luck, or fate would have it, the one student he least, and most, wanted to see was the one who now faced him. "Jade?" he asked.

"Yes, sir. Jade Simmons." Her lips were pink and pouty. "I was wondering something."

His hand gripped the eraser like a vice. "What?" he asked calmly. She was a prize.

"Well, sometimes I write very private things. I would show them to you, of course, since you're the teacher. But I don't want the rest of the class to see them. Would that be a problem?"

"Well, part of the class requirement is to share your work with your classmates and use them as your audience."

"But I'm not ready for an audience yet," she said softly. Her lashes lowered. She wore a bluejean jacket over a crisp white blouse rounded out by young breasts. Her skirt was very short, the color of summer skies. Beneath it she wore no stockings or pantyhose. Her golden, bare legs descended into the tops of short, black boots. Her hair was like a satin cape.

"Perhaps you can think of something new to write, which you won't be afraid to share," Dorian said, averting his gaze. It would be like touching warm wax to love this girl. But what was he thinking? After five years of teaching he'd never had such thoughts!

"Well, maybe," she answered. "But would you have time to look at some of the stuff I don't want to share? Please?"

"Aren't you embarrassed to show me?"

"Oh, no," she said. "I know *you* won't laugh. The other kids would, though. And I don't like to be laughed at." Her eyes deepened with the vehemence of her tone. They glimmered.

"Of course," he said gruffly. He turned away. "I'd be happy to look at any of your work. But make sure you write on the page which piece is okay to read aloud to the class, and which is not."

"I think when you see my poems, and my story, you'll know."

"That's fine," he said quickly. As he turned back to her he saw her smile. Her face was flushed again, a delicate shade of bronze.

He looked down.

"Thanks, Mr. Mayer!" She turned and was gone into the afternoon light. But a scent remained drifting through the air. Sweet apples on a summer day.

~

His fingers dug into the back of his neck as he sat at his desk. In front of him, on top of the pile of his students' new work, sat paper-clipped pages of poetry and one two page hand-written story all by the girl, Jade Simmons.

The top sheet contained a poem. The title: "Afternoon."

Dorian read the first line aloud, his voice a whisper in the still air of his office. "I lie on my stomach..."

He closed his eyes and rubbed at them with his palms. *I'm not ready for this,* he told himself. Another part of his mind said: *I'm a professional. I can do this without becoming personally involved.*

He opened his eyes and began to read again.

I lie on my stomach
on my little girl's bed
too big for dolls, now,
too young for a real man.
But my imagination
has always been strong.
Before me in the heated air

my fantasy appears
naked and craving my touch.
Outside my window
dusk drifts into night.
I am liquid with longing
as the sky grows
quietly purple.

When he finished he stared at the piece of paper for a long time. The poem was beautiful. Part of him hoped it would be bad. That Jade would have little or no talent and he could put his forbidden thoughts of her to rest, knowing she was just like the other kids, shallow and crude and dull. But it wasn't the case. This sixteen-year old showed a simple, raw talent with this one poem. His fingers sought the pages of the rest of her work.

The second poem was titled "Evening." It continued the thoughts of the first. And stirred him shamelessly.

He approaches me
and the night folds over us,
an erotic shadow.
His maleness is erect
and seeks my woman's heat.
My young hands touch him
everywhere.
My young hands like flowers
bloom against hard skin.
Hard and soft.
Soft and hard.
I remember a little song
my mother used to sing:
Love is like a dream
that brushes in your sleep.

The third poem went even further. It had no title.

He moves inside me
like a long, thick finger
probing for secrets.
But there are no secrets here.
Only the hot breaths of lovers
seeking the fabled world
of Eros.

Her story was called "The Virgin" and involved, in graphic detail, the seduction of a fifteen-year old by a nameless, adult man. Dorian could tell from the writing that Jade, though highly imaginative and obviously educated, was not writing from experience. He wrote a note at the end of the story telling her so.

~

"So," she said, approaching him after class. "You didn't like my story?"

Dorian turned. "I didn't say that, did I?"

"You said I wasn't experienced with the subject matter and it showed. But that was the point, wasn't it? My main character, after all, is a virgin."

Dorian made a pact right then and there that he was not going to blush. "Yes," he said quietly. "But it comes across that the author, not the character, is perhaps slightly naïve. You are so young to be writing about this subject, Jade." He smiled. "Haven't you written about anything else?"

She was frowning. "You mean cute poems about kittens and puppies and 'Why I Love America'?"

"No," Dorian said. "I don't mean that. But your true feelings."

She lowered her gaze. "Those are my true feelings." Her voice was shaky.

"All right," he said. "All right. But I was hoping that students in my class could learn to grow and expand their talents, not stay the same, not continue to write what they've already been writing in their little diaries for the past five years."

When she looked up at him, her eyes were filled with tears. "I can't write anything else. It's all I think about." Then she turned and ran from the room.

Dorian watched her push open the door with a shove, step onto the concrete still slippery from rain, and go down. Her hair whipped hard against her face, a black silk scarf.

He ran to the door and knelt at her side.

"I'm okay," she said, trying to stand while still holding onto her notebooks and texts.

He grabbed her arm. It was soft and smooth, like packed butter. "Are you sure?"

"Yes." Her voice quavered.

He could see the tears on her face. "Come on," he said. "I'll help you."

She stood but her ankle gave out and she would have fallen again if Dorian hadn't caught her.

"You've hurt your ankle. The nurse is gone for the day. How bad is it?"

"I sprained it a month ago. I just re-sprained it a little," she said. "It'll be fine."

"But you can't walk."

She sighed heavily.

"I'll have to call your parents," he said.

"They're in Hawaii. A second honeymoon."

"Can anyone come and get you?"

"No. I walk home every day."

Exasperated, he said the one thing he shouldn't have and it was out of his mouth before he could stop it. "I'll drive you."

She looked up at him with her tear-stained gaze so tender his heart stopped. "Thank you, Mr. Mayer."

~

In his car her scent pervaded. Honey and soap. Her hands were folded tightly in her lap and she looked straight ahead.

"Where do you live?" he asked as he started the engine.

"On Mulberry. Do you know it?"

He nodded. "Do you have anything you can put on your ankle?"

She shook her head. "I did. But my Ace bandage got eaten by the dog. Maybe you have one I could borrow?"

He stiffened. "At my house," he said.

"I don't mind if we stop there first. I'd like to see where you live."

"Jade, I..." He stopped, swallowed. "This is highly inappropriate, you know. Teachers and students should not be visiting each other's houses except in emergency."

"This is an emergency," she said.

He sighed. "Yes, I guess it is. We'll stop at my house first."

They parked in his gravel driveway and he undid his seatbelt. Jade looked up at him. "Can I come in?"

"I don't..." He looked at her pale, pleading eyes. "All right." He knew he'd regret it, but a part of him was so excited that reason was fading.

Whatever was between them was strong. Very strong. *And very bad*, he thought.

She sat on his couch while he took off her boot and the thin white sock underneath. Her foot was narrow and smooth. The ankle had swollen only a little. He touched it. "Does that hurt?"

She was staring at him with a look of longing that sent fire into him. "No," she said softly.

He tried to ignore her.

"Mr. Mayer?"

He glanced at her face again. "What?"

"Did you really like my story?"

"I like your work, yes, "he said quickly.

66

"And the poems?"

"The poems are very good for someone your age."

"What if I told you," she said slowly, her white front teeth coming forward and biting lightly at her lower lip, "if I told you I wasn't a virgin. Would it make a difference in how you read the story? And the poems?"

He cleared his throat and bent to wrap her ankle. "Maybe."

"How would it change things?"

"I don't know, Jade. Please stop asking me so many questions and let me wrap your ankle."

"I'm sorry."

He refused to look up. He could hear the pout in her voice and knew he wouldn't be able to stand that look. He was already crazy with notions of tearing off her clothes right there, ravishing her like a wild man. He concentrated on breathing deep and even.

After a few moments of silence, she said, "I am a virgin. So I guess my question was stupid, right?"

"No," he said. His hands fumbled with the bandage and it slid off so that he had to start all over again. "Hold still!" he yelled.

"But I didn't move," she protested, sniffling.

He shook his head and looked at her. More tears glimmered in her eyes. "I'm sorry. I'm just a klutz today. I didn't mean to yell at you."

"It's okay," she whispered.

He smiled and caught one of her tears as it fell from her pale eye. "Sweet thing," he murmured. "You don't know what you do to me."

"But I do..."

"Shh." He put a finger to her lips. "You can't say it. I'm your teacher."

"But we both feel it..."

He shook his head. "No! I could be fired."

"I'd never tell." The words floated on the air like a bad omen. His thoughts went black for a moment, then came back with more clarity.

"No."

She reached out and placed her hand on his cheek. "You wanted me that first day."

"No."

"I'm old enough to decide what I want for myself."

"You're sixteen."

"So?"

"You're a child."

"I don't have a child's body," she said.

"No, but you're too young. I could go to jail."

"I won't let you."

"Jade…"

Before he could stop her, she leaned forward and placed her lips on his. They were warm and yielding. Her mouth opened.

He backed away. "No."

Her lips followed. Forbidden nectar was so sweet. His mind reeled.

He couldn't stop his arms from going around her, couldn't keep his mouth shut. Gently, he embraced her lips with his and moved his mouth against her. She melted in his arms, her body pressing his.

On the floor of his living room, plush carpet cushioning their bodies, he set about deflowering her. The reasonable part of his mind was horrified. The emotional part was over-charged and more aroused than he'd ever felt in his life.

Her body was smooth and, except for a patch of dark pubic curls, completely hairless. The skylight overhead played strange light dances over her golden skin. Her hair caught the light and held it.

His own blond hair fell into his eyes. Everything happened as if it were a dream.

Jade moved sensuously like a cat. Her smooth body arched against him. Her shirt was off, and her bra, and her full, firm breasts curved like ripe, fresh fruit. He licked a rosy nipple and she gasped. He licked the other and elicited another gasp. He felt a sense of urgency, but forced himself to take his time with her.

A part of him didn't believe any of this was happening.

He didn't think, couldn't. His tongue lapped at her flat belly while his hands encased her narrow hips and pushed the last barriers away. Her skirt came off, and her silken panties. Now she was naked, and he could admire her at his leisure.

She was moaning, reaching for him. He let her embrace his still fully clothed body. She pushed at his shirt until he fumbled to take it off. Then her hand touched his groin. She looked up in question. "Can't I see you, too?"

Her pale eyes were innocent and lovely. He smiled and touched her face, kissing her on her parted lips. "Of course."

Her young hands undid the zipper, folded back the cloth. His underwear stretched tight across his erection. He pushed off the pants and looked at her. "Are you sure?"

She nodded.

He pulled the rest of his clothes off. She stared, wide-eyed. Finally, she whispered, "I've never seen a naked man before. Only pictures."

"It's not the same," he replied.

"No," she said. "It's not." She reached out and her fingers caressed his long hardness. "It's beautiful," she whispered, and he could only close his eyes and groan.

As he lay back on the carpet, her hands brushed against him like warm wind. The skylight flashed and he could tell by the deep gold of the light that the afternoon was waning. He wondered how late it was, but really didn't care.

Now both her hands were on him. Then he felt her lips caress the crown. His eyes shot open.

She grinned at him.

"Come here, you," he said to her, gathering her on top of him. His erection pushed between her parted legs. She undulated against it.

"You feel so good," she said. "Are you going to put it in me?"

"I don't think you're ready yet."

Her look was one of loss. "But..."

"I mean, not just this moment." He turned onto his side, depositing her on the rug. "Lie still," he said, sitting up. He was so hard that his penis stuck straight out, defying gravity. But he could wait.

"What are you going to do?"

"Make you ready," he said. He moved between her legs, covered her with his body and kissed her face. Then he moved his mouth slowly down. She cried out when his tongue touched between her legs. He parted the thighs further and licked deeply. She made little, sharp sounds and exclamations.

"Oh," she said, as he licked her sweetness. "I feel so, so full!"

She tasted like honey. He licked upward and tongued her clitoris. She arched and he caught her hips, pushing his mouth tighter against her. "Oh god," she said, "it feels so good!"

She writhed in his arms. Her entrance was so hot and slick now, that he knew she was close to orgasm, if she hadn't had a small one already.

He lifted his head. "I'm ready for you," he said softly.

"Oh yes," she said breathlessly. "Put it in me."

He stroked her slowly with his hand and she squirmed and moaned. He probed softly at the entrance to her body. She lifted her hips as if begging for more. He pressed in. She gasped. Then he slid all the way in and it was easier than he thought it was going to be.

"Does it hurt?" he asked, kissing her chin.

"No." Her eyes were closed. "Just full." She looked entranced.

She was tight and so hot on him that he knew he would not last more than a few minutes. He thrust slowly, trying to take his time, but it was so difficult.

After a few moments of this, he came so hard within her that he almost passed out.

She touched him afterwards and he never fully softened. He fingered her until she came again; she stroked him with her hands and then, later, her tongue. He came hard a second time right in her open palms. She was overcome with delight.

Afterwards, they lay together on the floor.

"What have I done, you sweet young thing," he said. "What have I done?"

"I won't tell, Mr. Mayer, I swear. I'll never tell."

"You could get pregnant," he said. "I wasn't even thinking."

"I'm on the pill. I was preparing myself for just such an occasion."

"Still, this was a stupid, stupid thing for me to do."

She hugged him tighter. "I swear, no one will ever find out."

But he thought about how autobiographical her writing was, and knew he was doomed to be immortalized on the pages of future assignments in future writing classes.

Sweet thing, he thought. *Oh delicate, dangerous creature.*

As he held her firm body against his, he stared into the skylight. He could see that the sun had already set. His penis stirred once more against her thigh as the sky grew quietly purple.

Child of Hermes, Child of Aphrodite

*"There are stars dancing
on the stage of the sky.
Some people call them
gods."*

Alon had curly, golden brown hair that framed his smooth face. His eyes looked like a faun's, rich brown and always shiny. He was, Noah guessed, about twenty-five or six, and had the most svelt and graceful body of all the dancers in the show.

Night after night, as the curtain rose and the footlights came up, Alon danced beside Noah and the ten other members of the chorus. Though Noah never missed a step or a cue, his mind was only half on his work. Alon obsessed him. His concentration was interrupted constantly by that black and silver clad body that stepped in tune with his, the sweat-glistened stomach which his costume left bare, the slim, cat-like muscles of his arms.

Alon spoke to him only occasionally, as did the other dancers, to inquire about this costume change or that, to compliment for a night's job well-done, to say hello or good-bye. Other than that, he seemed not to notice Noah's infatuation. Or if he did notice, he ignored it. And Noah was, for once in his life, too shy to outwardly extend the conversations in order to pursue him.

Noah didn't know what to do.

Though many dancers in the industry were known to be bisexual, social etiquette demanded he not make that stereotypical assumption. Dancers were sensitive types, and the straight ones hated being thought of as gay just as the gay ones hated the notion that same-sex preference might be expected of them. Noah himself was bi and had just broken up with a girl he'd been seeing for two years. He was tired of women, for the time-being, so it was natural for him to be interested in, and attracted to the men on his team. Some were obviously gay, and he would have had no trouble making a 'catch' of any one of them. But none interested him like Alon. And night after night this dancer who had magicked him moved beside him like a shadow he couldn't touch.

He'd asked around, slyly, subtly, and no one seemed to know anything about Alon, whether he was gay, straight or bi, whether he'd worked on Broadway before, whether he was under 25, or over.

The mystery deepened and Noah, two weeks into a show that was getting rave reviews, started to lose sleep because of strange dreams populated by Alon that both disturbed and aroused him during the morning hours when he tried to sleep.

The unanswered questions about Alon haunted him. He'd arrive at work with dark circles under his eyes. Make-up helped to hide the effects of his sleeplessness, but his dancing, though flawless, had lost some of its verve.

"Whatever's bugging you," the director said to him, taking him aside one night, "you'd better take care of it. You're okay now but I can tell you're straining for those final leaps. You're not concentrating. Lack of concentration leads to injury. And then you'll be finished in this career. Understand?"

"Yes," Noah said. "I promise, I'll take care of it."

After the pep talk, he decided to take the risk of rejection and approach Alon. Rejection would be difficult to live with, what with the after effect of having to continue to face the man every day. But living with this obsession was equally as difficult. It would be like trading an apple for an orange.

He wasn't normally a shy man, but his obsession made him giddy. The thought of confessing his inner feelings to a man who could crush him by the simple word "no" weakened his resolve. But the director was right. His career was at stake if he didn't take care of his mental anguish. And seeing Alon, talking to him instead of obsessing on all those 'what ifs' confusing his mind was the only way.

The dressing room was, as usual, full of men. The male extras on the show, as well as the male members of the chorus which had eight men and only four women, all shared the long room and the bulb-framed make-up mirrors which lined two walls.

Noah entered, brushing past a half-dressed black man named Sergei who jumped and almost fell back, long legs tangled in the pants he'd been struggling to get on.

"Sorry," Noah murmured, moving past.

"No problem, man," his fellow dancer added. "Why are you in such a hurry?"

Noah pretended not to hear him. The air was scented with the perfume of facial powders, grease-paint, hair-sprays and deodorants. There were spicy smells mixed with sweet smells. Like a fog, the scents clung to his mouth and throat.

He could see Alon standing toward the back of the long room. The mirrors reflected him twice. His gold-brown skin shined like dark copper. He wore the shiny, tight spandex pants of his costume and nothing else. His bare arms and chest, firm and hairless, gleamed.

Noah's throat went dry. The man was too beautiful to talk to, too horribly attractive for Noah to be near him and retain any semblance of sanity. That he could continue, nightly, to perform beside this satyr was somewhat of a minor miracle. But the idea of talking to him—real person to real person—was expecting too much.

The director's words came back to him then, sharp needles on his mind. *You'll be finished in this career.* That gave him incentive. And somehow his feet kept moving. Somehow he managed to elbow his way to Alon's side and remain alive, valid, still breathing. Another minor miracle.

Noah cleared his throat. "Hey, I need to talk to you," he said, almost too loudly, though the din in the room was always an excited roar.

Alon turned. "Me?" he asked, one long, golden finger pointing to his chest. His dark painted eyebrows rose. The soft brown eyes, framed by black eyeliner, glowed with a dusky, inner beauty that threatened to stop Noah's heart. The shiny curls that crowned his head were dusted with glitter.

They were of a same height, about six feet, and Noah found himself staring squarely into that so smooth, beardless face with the reddened lips, gleaming teeth, damp brown eyes. His lungs quivered. "Yes." he finally said. "You."

"Sure," Alon said casually. "Just let me change first." He turned away and bent to remove the Spandex. Noah tried to look away but couldn't. He swallowed tightly as Alon worked the tight costume over his hips revealing tight, rounded buttocks, golden as the rest of him and with no sign of a tan line.

Alon's profile showed he wore a tight g-string with a single strap that hugged his waist, a string that delved into the crevice between his buttocks, and a black pouch that gathered his genitals into a firm, round pocket of flesh.

Noah's skin began to sweat. He already had on his sweats over his costume, intending to wear it home and wait for privacy to take it off and jump into the shower. He was always erect after a show and it somewhat embarrassed him, so it was common practice for him to keep his costume on. He'd already hastily wiped his make-up off in the bathroom, so there was nothing left to do but wait, awkwardly, while Alon readied himself for the outer world beyond the footlights, mirror-lights and stage.

To Noah's relief, Alon was quick. His grey sweats went on smoothly over his g-string and he cinched them with deft hands. He put on a black sweatshirt with cut-off sleeves, slipped on tennis shoes that had no laces, grabbed a slim ski jacket from the chair-back and turned. "Okay," he said. "I'm done."

Noah blinked and had to smile. "Your make-up," he said softly.

Alon turned to face himself in the mirror. "Oh, yeah. It'll take just a minute." He sat down and grabbed a jar of cold cream. One hand smeared it over his face, the other pulled wads of tissue from a box.

He did an incomplete job. When he stood, Noah could still see traces of the eyeliner. Glitter flickered sporadically in his hair. But his face was clean now, not quite as shiny, not quite as tan. He looked fantastic.

"Okay?" Alon asked, eyebrows raised.

Noah shrugged and glanced at his hands. "Sure."

"So, where do you want to go to talk?" he asked as Noah led the way out of the still crowded dressing room. "And what's this all about anyway? You've barely said two words to me the whole time we've been dancing together."

Once they were outside in the dim shadows of backstage, Noah relaxed a little. "I don't know where to go. But I need to talk. It's important."

Alon stood to the side, hands on his hips, jacket thrown over his shoulder. "Well, hell, I don't have any money on me but some change. I wasn't planning on going out tonight. But we could get a cup of coffee, I guess. I like coffee after a show. It sort of revives me."

"I have coffee at my apartment," Noah said, immediately damning himself for being so forward. Then he added, "It's free."

Alon shrugged. "Sure. I guess that's okay. If you don't mind. Where do you live?"

Noah told him and Alon, who walked home every night because he lived so close to the theatre, said he didn't have money for a cab.

"Don't worry about it. I've got money," Noah said.

"Well, then I'll have to borrow some to get home," Alon said. "Why don't we walk to my apartment instead? I have coffee there."

Noah hesitated. He'd be off his turf. This was so awkward for him anyway. Now he'd be really putting Alon on the spot if he confessed his feelings in the man's own apartment.

"I don't mind," Alon said. "Honestly." He smiled. "You have me intrigued."

Noah groaned and, turning away, put a hand to his eyes. Seduction was difficult enough for him. He didn't need added embarrassment to compound that difficulty.

"C'mon," Alon said, moving toward the exit. "Whatever it is, it can't be that bad."

Noah followed.

As they walked down the midnight street, the streetlights and traffic made it almost look like day. The night was cool but not overly so. Alon carried his jacket.

"I think tonight was one of our best shows," Alon commented.

"Yeah."

"You did great," he added. "Your performance is always flawless."

"So is yours," Noah said.

"Ah, well, I have tremendous concentration. In most things in life, I'm so easily distracted. I never did get good grades in school because of it."

"But dancing is different," Noah said.

"Definitely. It's as if I become another person."

The manhole covers on the street were spewing steam. It fogged the air and evaporated in a series of ghost-dances. Noah walked beside Alon and felt displaced.

"I was old when I started to dance. Sixteen."

"I was five," Noah said.

"I wish I'd started earlier, but it never occurred to me until the first time I saw a Broadway show. Now, here I am."

"Have you been in other shows?" Noah asked.

"Only two. One on Hollywood. One off-Broadway. I moved here last year."

"So this is your first Broadway show? That's great."

"I'm happy about it, "Alon said.

They walked for five more minutes before turning into a building and going through the glass doors. Alon pushed the elevator button for up. When they got in he pushed for the fourth floor.

Alon's apartment was small and neat. He had nice stereo equipment, a leather couch, a big screen TV and lots of plants.

"Relax," he said, nodding toward the couch. "I'll start the coffee."

Noah sat, pushing his long legs straight out in front of him. He wore black sweats and tennis shoes over his Spandex costume. Over the top he had on a white sweatshirt. Suddenly, he felt overly warm.

"Hey." Alon's voice drifted from the kitchen. "Make yourself at home." Then he came around the wall that separated the living room from the kitchen. "You look hot in that sweatshirt. Take it off if you like."

"Thanks." Noah shrugged out of it. His black and silver costume top which left his stomach bare was drenched in sweat. He was embarrassed yet again, and used the shirt to try to mop some of the excess liquid from his skin. His fingers combed back the dark bangs of his hair. Feathered in front and long in back, it stuck to his neck in tendrilled clumps.

Alon came back into the room and plopped down on the other end of the couch. "It'll be a few minutes," he said. "Mr. Coffee's warming up."

"That's fine," Noah said.

Alon nodded and stared at him. "You were planning on going right home, too," he said looking at Noah's costume top. "What's wrong? What changed your mind?"

Noah stared at his lap, then forced himself to look up and meet Alon's alluring eyes. The traces of eyeliner were still discernable and gave him that exotic look that had obsessed Noah from the beginning. "I…uh, I had a little chat with the director tonight."

Alon leaned forward, concern narrowing his brows. "What about?"

"My performance."

"What about it? It's flawless. Everyone knows that."

"It's strained. And it shows."

"Since I dance right beside you, I'm willing to give you any help you need. That's why you wanted to talk to me, right? Because I'm the closest to you in the line?"

"Sort of," Noah said, swallowing hard again.

"So, why do you think your performance is strained?"

Noah let out a sharp breath. It sounded like a bitter laugh. "If I tell you I'm afraid you'll throw me out of here on my ass. But I have to tell you."

"Tell me what?" Alon's gaze was interested and innocent.

"It's you that's interfering with my concentration." Noah couldn't look at him now. "I'm so damnably attracted to you, I can't think straight. Now go ahead and throw me out on the street. I deserve it. And I won't hold it against you."

Alon said nothing for a long while. Noah waited.

Finally the couch moved. Out the corner of his eye, Noah saw Alon lean back and scratch his head. "I'm not going to throw you out," he said quietly.

Noah turned. Alon was staring straight ahead.

"But I can't go to bed with you, either," Alon added after a few seconds.

"Oh, I understand. You're straight. That's fine. I…I just needed to talk about it, that's all," Noah said, stumbling over the words and flushing.

"It's not that I'm straight. It's not that at all. It's just that I don't do that sort of thing very often. I just don't."

"It's all right," Noah said quickly. "I'm sorry." He stood. "I'm really sorry. I should go."

"No." Alon sat forward. "Sit back down. I want you to stay. Have that cup of coffee with me. We need to talk. You need to talk."

Feeling all the strength give out in his knees, Noah sat back down.

Alon stood. "I'll go get the coffee. Black?"

"Yeah." Noah could only stare after him as he rounded the path into the kitchen.

He couldn't think. His vision was blurred. Why was he staying here to further embarrass himself? And yet, why was he embarrassed? Alon seemed very accepting. He hadn't expected to really jump the guy. He'd wanted to just talk. Now Alon wanted to talk. With those thoughts, he forced himself to relax. He concentrated on slowing his heart.

Minutes later Alon returned with two mugs. He handed one to Noah. "Black as space," he said, smiling. "Whereas, I take everything in mine." He placed the cup on a low, wood coffee table and sat, turning to face Noah.

"So," Alon began, "why don't you start by relaxing. I'm not mad at you. I don't want you to feel embarrassed. I'm actually glad you came to me."

"I'm just being stupid," Noah said.

"Why say that?"

"About a month ago I broke up with my girlfriend of two years. I'm feeling kinda off women right now. My eye's been roving toward men. It's stupid of me to be distracted by something like physical attraction. I'm a big boy now. I ought to be able to control myself."

"Your girlfriend," Alon said. "Did she leave you for someone else?"

Noah took a small sip of his coffee. It burned the tip of his tongue. "Don't they all?" He leaned forward and placed the full mug on the coffee table.

"Maybe that's why you're feeling a little out of control. Anger, hurt, resentment, jealousy can do that."

Noah rubbed at his forehead. "I guess."

"I'm bi, too," Alon said abruptly.

"That's great," Noah said, but his voice showed he didn't feel the words.

80

"Look, your girlfriend hurt you real bad. I'd just be the rebound, right? It's not worth it."

Noah turned to face him. "I don't think so," he said. Damn the man was beautiful!

Alon ducked his head. "Really, you don't even know me. We dance together every night, that's all."

Noah gripped his own pant leg. "I think I'm losing it. You're all I ever think about."

"You're lying!" He punctuated the statement with a laugh.

"It's true. I know I'm putting you on the spot..."

"No," Alon interrupted. "I think you're cute, too. Really. I'm very easily attracted to you. I'd go with you in a second, but there're some things you don't understand."

Noah frowned. "You would?" Shock shot through him like lightning.

"Yeah. You're a great guy. I love dancing beside you. You got a beautiful body and deep eyes, mysterious. I like that. But I just..." He stopped.

"I don't believe you're saying this. You can't mean it."

"I do. But I have a few things about me that, well, frankly make me steer clear of the bedroom most of the time. I don't like the way people treat me in there. I don't usually like sex."

Noah gulped. "You don't like sex?"

"No," Alon said. "Not usually. At least not with another person." He chuckled nervously.

"But why? Have people hurt you?"

"Some," Alon said.

"How?"

He stared up at the ceiling. "How? Well, in many ways."

Noah folded his hands tightly in his lap. "And you think I would."

"I don't know if you would. I'm shy about my body and a lot of people don't understand that."

"You're shy about your body? You? A dancer? You changed clothes right in front of me in the dressing room."

Alon smiled. "I'm shy about my body in conjunction with sex."

"Because people have hurt you?" This was like a puzzle and Noah was determined to figure it out.

"Partly."

"I don't understand."

"I know you don't."

Noah nodded. "But you don't want to explain. Well then, why don't you tell me it's none of my business?"

"I haven't had a relationship the whole time I've been living here. Maybe it's time I tried."

Noah held his breath.

"I like you," Alon continued. "But I'm afraid you won't like me."

"I do like you," Noah protested. "I already like you. I'm obsessed by you."

"I mean if I did decide to go to bed with you, I'm afraid you wouldn't like me afterwards."

"Why? Do you bite?"

Alon did not smile. He shook his head and bowed it.

"What can I say? What promise do you want from me?" Noah asked. "I'd do anything for you. My dancing is suffering. I have nothing more to give. If you allow me to give you all of that, why then would you think I'd not like you afterwards?"

Alon sighed loudly. He said nothing.

"Do you want me to leave?" Noah asked.

Alon shook his head.

"Well, then tell me. Why do you say those things? What have people done to you?"

"People are cruel," he said, standing. He turned to Noah and reached out his hand. "Come here. I'm going to show you something."

Noah couldn't resist. He reached up and stood. Alon's hand was warm in his, and moist. He led him through the living room without a word and into a tiny hall. At the end a door opened onto a bedroom with black, white and blue furnishings. One entire wall was a mirror. The bed was huge and full. Piled at the head on the black spread were white, blue and black pillows. Off to the right was a bathroom. Alon led him there. At the door to the bathroom, he stopped, let go of Noah's hand and faced him. "Now," he said.

"What?" Noah asked, still confused.

Alon's hands went to the string at this waist that held up the sweats. He undid it and they fell.

"Shit," Noah said. "What are you trying to do, drive me crazy?"

Alon shook his head. "Don't talk. I have to show you."

"But..."

"Don't talk," Alon said firmly. "Please. Just let me show you." There were traces of tears in his eyes.

Noah closed his mouth.

By the bathroom door was a panel of switches. Alon flipped them up. The room lit with a day-like glow. A lamp on the ceiling spotlighted the bed. Alon kicked aside his laceless shoes and the sweats, and moved toward the bed. Wearing only the cut-off sweatshirt and black g-string, he sat on the edge. Looking up at Noah, he said, "Come here."

Noah couldn't breathe. His heart was in his throat. He approached with painful steps. His penis jutted achingly against his costume. The man was utterly turning him on. But if it wasn't a seduction, what could it be?

When he faced him, Alon hooked his fingers into his waistband, then lifted his hips and slipped the g-string off in one fluid motion. He tossed it aside. His penis, medium-sized and half-erect, was like a pink finger point at him from a thatch of brown curls. Noah stared. It was beautiful, but there was something different about it.

"Look at me," Alon said.

Noah lifted his gaze to meet the other's worried face. "I am. You're beautiful."

"You're not seeing it all."

"What?" Noah glanced down again.

Alon leaned back on the bed and spread his legs. With his left hand, he grasped his penis and pulled it up. "There," he said. "Now you know why."

Noah stared. What he saw at first didn't register. The bright light left little to the imagination. Below Alon's penis there was no sac, no testicles, only a small raised lump and below that, the soft folds of a vulva. There was an opening. It was not an anus. That was further down.

Noah's jaw dropped. "You have both," he exclaimed.

Alon clasped his legs together and sat up. His left palm covered his male organ. His other arm pressed against his stomach. "Now you know," he said. "Most people can't handle that," he said. "Freaks 'em out."

Noah, still staring at Alon's handsome face, was speechless. His knees buckled. He landed on them hard, putting his hand out to the carpet to catch himself.

"I don't usually do that to people. Maybe I just felt like shocking someone for a change." His voice was bitter.

Noah took a deep breath. "You did that," Noah managed to say. "But I...I don't understand those others. I think...," he gulped, "I think you're beautiful!"

Alon hunched into himself. "No you don't. No one does. So please just go."

The words stabbed him in the chest. "No. It's true. You're lovely. It's wonderful. You have the best of both—"

"Don't say it!" Alon said angrily. "Just don't! I don't fit in anywhere. Straight women hate it. Gay men hate it. And vice versa."

"But I'm not like them," Noah said. He reached out to Alon's knee. Alon slapped his hand away. Tears in his eyes were catching the light in angry flickers.

"Once," he said, "I was with a bisexual man who said that I was beautiful, that he liked it. I'd only been with women before, so I was a virgin in a sense. I told him not to, but he

84

put it in me. He hurt me. I'm smaller than normal women there. But he didn't care. I bled. I never saw him again."

"That's rape," Noah said softly.

"Damn right it is!" Alon swatted at the tears that started to fall. "Shit."

"Hey," Noah said. He reached out again. Alon tried to push him away but Noah forced the issue. He moved up so that he was sitting next to him, on arm around his shoulders. "Let me stay. Please," he whispered.

"I hate sex," Alon said, sniffling.

"I won't have sex with you, then. I'll just stay with you." Noah couldn't believe his own words. His erection was so stiff that it hurt.

"I hate sex," Alon said again.

Noah held him. After awhile, the man relaxed in his arms. He pillowed his head on Noah's shoulder. Minutes of silence passed. The bright light was a glare. The warmth of Alon against his side increased. Noah closed his eyes.

Finally, Alon moved. He raised his head. "Hey," he said, pulling at the elastic strap on Noah's shoulder. "I took off my clothes. Now you have to."

Noah frowned. "I'm embarrassed."

"Why?"

"I'm so hard it hurts."

Alon chuckled. "I can take care of that."

"But—"

"I know, I know. I said I hate sex. I like giving blow jobs, though."

"No." Noah shook his head.

"Why?" Alon looked hurt.

"Because I wanted to share myself with you, not use you. So I'll just keep my clothes on, okay?"

Alon sat back. His eyes were still damp around the lashes. The left-over eyeliner had smeared. "No one's ever said that to me before. Hell, I've never known a guy to turn down a blow job."

Noah shrugged. "I told you I'm not like those others who hurt you."

"Yeah, I guess you did."

"So, why don't you put your clothes back on and we'll think of something else to do."

Alon stared at him for a few seconds, then leaned forward and kissed him on the lips. Noah responded by gently parting his mouth. When Alon pulled back, he was breathless. "I think you're a godsend," he said.

"I think you're a god," Noah replied.

"Take off your clothes," Alon said again.

With Alon's help, Noah's clothes came away quickly and easily. Alon shrugged out of his shirt. The two men faced each other, erections bobbing. They embraced.

"I come like a man," Alon whispered in his ear. "My testicles are inside. But I can come like a woman, too, if you use your tongue just right."

Noah's vision dizzied and blurred. He pushed the man gently to the mattress and kissed him. "How delightful," he answered.

Alon reached between them and touched Noah's penis. Noah groaned. "You're so hard," he said.

Noah nodded.

"Let me help." Alon pushed Noah onto his back. Their flesh rubbed. Alon's skin was smooth as marble, his dancer's physique firm and silky. He ran his hands over his chest, down the sides and gently touched the pink organ between his legs. Then the organ was out of his reach as Alon moved between Noah's legs. His hands caressed and explored. He cupped Noah's testicles and gently squeezed. Noah's cock bobbed and swelled. He closed his eyes tight.

After a moment, he felt wet heat engulf him. Alon's mouth moved down his length, a slick pressure. He cried out.

Alon sucked at him in a way no one ever had. He knew exactly what brought the most pleasure. The tongue moved to tickle the underside of his penis, the teeth rubbed lightly and the whole mouth was like a vacuum pulling him in.

White light in his mind blinded him as he came. Alon sucked at his throbbing erection as it burst with seed. He felt the man swallow and swallow. Alon didn't stop until he was dry.

When it was over, Alon moved up in the bed and embraced him. "Is that what you wanted?" he asked.

Noah turned lethargically to face him. "I wanted you. Any way. Every way. I don't care."

Alon smiled. "When you're ready, I'll do it again."

"Will you let me do that for you?" Noah asked.

Alon glanced away. Noah caught his face in his hands and turned it toward him. He leaned forward and kissed him. "How can I convince you?" he said, pulling back, "that I love how you look. That I want you. Not what you are, but who you are. How can I?"

"You do convince me, Noah. It's just that I've been so hurt."

"I know." Noah pulled him close. He let Alon rest his curly head on his chest and stroked his back in slow circles. The circles moved lower until he cupped well-rounded buttocks with his open palms. His free hand delved between them. He kissed Alon on the forehead and touched the penis that pressed between them. "Let me," he whispered. "Oh, please let me."

Alon's eyes were closed. He said nothing. Noah's palm curved around the hard length and stroked gently upward. "I want you to feel good," he kept repeating. "I just want you to feel good."

His hand delved below the penis and petted the delicate folds of skin there. One finger slipped between the lips. There was a slickness. He coated his finger and continued to rub.

Finally, Alon began to squirm. The arousal was taking over and his body moved with it. He rolled onto his back, legs spread, knees bent.

Slowly, with his hand still rubbing both penis and vulva, Noah kissed his way down the smooth chest and belly, skin like polished leather, warm and tan. His lips descended first on the penis, which seemed to reach for him with a life of its own. He heard Alon gasp, felt the gentle thrust as the penis pushed deeper into his mouth. He sucked hard, then moved up and down again and again, increasing the pace. His forefinger teased the folds beneath it.

Alon's erection stood straight up when Noah lifted his mouth off it. He lowered his head. His tongue lapped at the dampness between the lips of that second set of genitals, tongue finding a tiny bud, lips closing around it and sucking. With the tip of his tongue, he thrust into the tiny opening that was, as Alon said, smaller than a normal woman's, and very sweet and pink. His hand stroked the hard cock, his tongue tasted beneath and, when he thought he could do this forever, Alon gasped and cried out, "Noah!"

Noah's hand tightened on his cock. He licked at the bumps beneath it which were, he guessed, the inner testes, licked up the side and sucked in the head.

The penis swelled, throbbed, then spurted warm liquid from its tip. Noah milked it with his hand and went back to the folds of skin below. He licked and sucked there, as Alon continued to orgasm. He moaned and squirmed and thrust himself against Noah's hand, his face.

Later, they slept with their arms tightly embracing one another.

The next night, when they performed, they danced side by side infused with pure joy, in complete rapport, and with flawless conception. The thousands of eyes that watched shared in their pleasure.

Robot Love

"As if there could be something like
Intimacy between us, as if I could ever
Communicate anything so mysterious,
Anything so austere and familiar
As even this simple story, written down..."

-Edward Hirsch, "A Dark Hillside"

I can report only what transpired without emotional response, for I have no true feelings of my own.

Since you have requested a log of my past day's activities, I record here, in the order they occurred, the events of the day and night of my employment in the house of Corinna Alexandria Dannon, human female, age: 32. I omit only repetitive details, as programmed, so that the log is less a transcript and more a narrative journey through the late hours of May first and the early hours of the second, 2092.

I arrive at the time specified by the agency, 6 P.M. Corinna Alexandria Dannon's house is large, by city standards, with an approximate six foot wide concrete spread that makes up the front yard, and two foot sidewalks that lead to the back. The small porch is elevated. I take two steps up and stand upon a silver mat that blinks **WELCOME** in large amber letters. The doorbell is a flat square of light where I place my palm. I can hear faint strains of wind chimes sounding within.

Corinna Alexandria Dannon opens the front door and, upon seeing me, gasps, puts her hand to her lips and states, "But you're beautiful!"

"I am called Stiel," I reply. "You should not be surprised. You requested this form."

"Come in," she says, taking me by the hand. "You can call me Cory."

"Thank you, Cory."

Cory's interior decorating is of a haphazard design all her own. She has a throw rug by the front door which appears to be made from plastic and silk. Its color scheme is red and black. The walls of her front room, which she calls her living room, are pale purple. Abstract collages, which she has created herself, hang from the walls. I do not understand them, but acknowledge that they give her great pleasure. This is fulfilling to me, as my programming is strictly for pleasure and anything which facilitates that is a most welcome addition to my core of information.

A video screen is encased in one wall. She informs me she has not been able to afford the new popular style of reconstructing the entire wall to make one, gigantic screen. I tell her that for myself it is not a necessity that the wall be a screen. I watch videos only for information and can get that information just as easily from a small screen as a large one.

She laughs and my programming is satisfied.

I am then given a tour of the home. We leave the unique living room and its worn and patched artificial leather furniture and enter the kitchen. She shows me the appliances and where the food is kept. The kitchen is white and brown with chrome inlays of ancient Aztec designs. It is, like the living room, quite unique.

"Do you eat?" Cory asks.

"I can eat certain foods," I reply. "I can ingest water, bread, some soups and desserts. I cannot put into my system any carbonated or alcoholic beverages. They would greatly debilitate my life-span. As would fresh fruits, except for bananas."

"Good," she says, "because I'm getting hungry and I don't want to eat alone. Again." She turns away.

"I shall be happy to cook for you," I say. As programmed, my culinary knowledge is extensive.

As we tour the rest of the house, Cory shows me the bathroom and single bedroom. Truly a large accommodation,

90

by city standards, for one person. She claims she was lucky to get it.

The colors of the bedroom and bathroom are white and blue. Blue, she tells me, is her favorite color. We discuss the various shades, which I shall not bother to reiterate, and walk back to the kitchen where I prepare spaghetti with artificial meat sauce for her dinner.

While I cook, she tells me a little about herself. She begins with a statement that is, to my programming, a non-sequitur.

"I hate men."

"All men?" I ask.

She nods and her hair, which is long and the color known as Jeral golden blonde, falls over her shoulders and brushes her face. She is a small woman. I estimate her weight at 117 or 118. Her eyes are a slate shade of gray. Her face is small and round. I do not know if she is pretty, because the concept is not one I am able to judge, but from my observations I can state with assurance her appearance is not abnormal. Men should find her a suitable mate. Why, then, this hatred for the opposite sex?

I ask her just that.

"They want only one thing. And they are never loyal," she says.

"What one thing?"

"Why sex, of course."

I say nothing because my programming is based on just such an act. Sex and giving pleasure are my primary functions. If she dislikes those aspects of me, then I will be a failure in my role.

"What I mean is," she goes on to explain, "is that their need for sex makes them unfaithful. They're assholes, that's all."

"Has such an occurrence recently happened?"

"Recently?" She laughs. "Shit, it's happened all my life. Every guy I've ever known has left me. For another woman."

"That must be quite disturbing," I reply.

91

"Yeah, well, that's why I finally decided to do away with them for good. If I want sex, I can damn well buy it! So, that's why you're here." She shrugs.

"It is one of my many functions," I say.

She stares at me for about ten seconds, then says as she breathes slowly out, "Damn you're beautiful."

The compliment is eminently satisfying to my programming. I am designed to appear as a six foot two inch human male with firm musculature about the shoulders and chest, narrow hips and long legs. I have no body hair except on my head and over my eyes (eyebrows.) My hair is brown and wavy. It is collar length and warm to the touch.

At Cory's request before I came, I dressed casually. The bleached black jeans I wear are torn at the hem. The first three buttons on my white shirt are undone. The attire is extremely beneficial for all movement including walking, sitting, cooking.

The opinion that I am beautiful is simply that, an opinion. But it is important that Cory thinks I am. It offers me the possibility that my job will be error free.

At dinner, I eat bare noodles and drink water from the tap. Cory eats the meat sauce and compliments me on the flavor. If I could be pleased, I might be insufferable.

After dinner we watch a video called *Looking For Night*. It is a love story set in the future. Parts of it depict graphic sex which my programming always finds interesting. Since sex between humans is my focus, I carefully study those scenes. They show me nothing I have not already seen or tried, but the facial reactions interest me, though I know the people are only actors. When men achieve orgasm, which cannot be realistically faked, their faces are rapt. Because that response is true and not part of the acting process, I am drawn by my programming to watch those parts again and again. I myself, of course, feel nothing when I trigger orgasmic response. I do it for the sole pleasure of my partner. But I study the facial mannerisms in order to copy them for myself. I am driven by my functions to be as fully human in response as possible. I learn by observation.

From little signs, such as accelerated breathing, pink-tinged skin and tenser than normal muscles, I can tell Cory is erotically stimulated by the movie. I touch her thigh.

She turns to me and smiles. "What do you think?" she asks.

"I think that they are very good at what they do. But I am better."

"Oh, really? You're not modest, are you, Stiel?"

"Not unless modesty would bring you further pleasure."

She giggles. "No. I like a confident man. Just not arrogant."

"I have nothing to be arrogant about because I have no emotions. But I assure you my physical stimulation programming is superb. It was reviewed in the Yorkish Weekly and given the top rating."

"Five stars, I know," Cory says. "And that's why you're here."

I smile down at her. "Yes, it is."

She is obviously delighted, for even before the movie ends she is fondling me. I kiss her softly on the mouth and stroke her still-clothed breasts.

"If I suck you, will you get hard?" she asks me as I pull back my mouth.

"Yes."

"Can I? It turns me on so much to do that to a guy."

"Of course. Do you want to do this here? In your living room."

"Yeah," she answers. "Right here."

"That is quite acceptable."

She loosens the buttons on my jeans and pulls out my organ. She bends over my lap and her lips cover the head. Though I can feel nothing, my receptors respond and warm it.

"Mmm," she says between licks. "You taste real."

"I am meant to," I reply, my hands caressing her hair.

She wets me very thoroughly and as her head moves up and down, I can see actors doing the very same thing in the movie that is still playing on the screen. The male leans back while the female fellates him. His penis is thick and flushed.

My own grows, too, in rhythm with Cory's moving mouth. I do not need this sort of stimulation to become hard, but Cory enjoys it so I let her go on as long as she wishes.

The actor on the screen, black hair in his eyes, is tossing his head back and forth. The actress moves faster upon him. I know he is going to orgasm because of the tightness of his testicles, the grimace of his mouth, his eyes clenched shut. When he does, the arc of sperm lands in his lover's hair. Some spills down the sides of his organ. The female licks him clean and the scene fades.

"Can you, if I want you to, come in my mouth?"

I look down. Cory stares up at me. "If you want me to," I reply.

"What's it like?" she asks. "For you."

"It is satisfaction in the fulfillment of my program. Mental satisfaction only, but it is all I require."

"Then do it."

"Very well." I lean back and order up the response. She moves back down on my organ and continues to fellate me.

I allow myself to swell and harden to my full length. As Cory's mouth comes off me, then starts again to descend, I let the building liquid come forth. She swallows it and me. I throw back my head and imitate the facial response of the actor in the movie.

After I am depleted, the organ softens. Cory sits up. "You can get hard again, can't you?"

"At a moment's notice," I reply. "What do you wish?"

"Everything."

I nod. I surmise she wishes me to take charge. "First we begin by divesting you of your clothes."

She chuckles and blushes. "I love the way you talk."

94

She, also, is wearing jeans. I undo the top button and grab her shirt where it is tucked in and pull. Then I raise it over her head. She helps by lifting her arms.

Next I undo the tiny bra she wears. It is white and lacy. First I kiss the lace where it touches her skin, then I unclasp the garment and expose her breasts. They are small but bounce as they are released. I take the left one, nipple and all, into my mouth and suck. Cory's intake of breath is a hiss. I mouth it for several seconds before turning to the one on the right. She arches against my mouth.

My hands move to her jeans again, and undo the rest of the buttons. Slowly I push them over her hips. I move my mouth from her breasts to her sternum and lick. My hands push her jeans all the way off. She is left wearing only panties. I notice the entire crotch is missing. "Do you want to keep these on?" I whisper into her ear.

She moans and nods.

She is small so it is easy for me to lift her and position her the way I think she will like. I sit her in my lap and stroke her all over. She tenses every time I touch the thatch of hair above her vulva. I sense she is ready for more.

I direct her back onto the couch and, still seated, place her legs so that I am between them. The folds of her vulva are dark and perfectly framed above and below by her crotchless white underwear. I bend down and touch the lips of her genitals lightly with my tongue. She makes noises that tell me she is feeling only pleasure.

I use my hands to hold the outer lips open as I lick and suck at the tender bud of her clitoris and probed with my tongue at the entrance to her body. My tongue registers dampness and warmth. I place my hands underneath her, fingers encountering panty silk, and lift her to my mouth for better access. She moans and her head tosses on the worn cushion of the couch.

"Oh, Stiel," she cries out. "You're going to make me come."

She doesn't fight me or stop me so I continue to tease her, to press her body to my mouth. With my tongue delving into the opening to her vagina, I can gather the rich moistness of her pleasure on the tip and spread it upwards. She cries out and I know the orgasm has arrived. I suck down on her clitoris the way I've been taught to draw all feeling out of the person, and she rocks against me and moans. Her thighs tense and clutch my head. I know for the moment she has lost all sense of reality and doesn't realize she is squeezing so hard. It does not disturb my programming in the least.

After I lift my head from her she sits up. "I want you in me," she says.

"Of course." But before I can move, she straddles my lap. I quickly make my organ hard. She positions herself over it and it enters her body in a smooth, long stroke.

The movie has now ended. The screen is dark. The room is more shadowed without that light. It is more conducive to this sort of exercise, says my programming. But Cory doesn't even seem to notice.

For awhile she stays that way, moving a little up and down, but mostly touching my face and chest with small, pale hands, kissing my face and mouth, petting my hair.

"I want to do this with you all night," she whispers.

"All right," I say.

She smiles and leans her head into the crook of my neck. I hold her and thrust gently into her.

After awhile I can see the pleasure beginning to build in her again. Her skin has a sparkly sheen of sweat. Her eyes, half-closed, glow with an inner heat.

"I want you to ravish me," Cory says suddenly. "Take me hard and fast."

"I'd love to ravish you," I reply.

I take her in my arms and turn her onto the couch. With her back pressed against the cushions, and her knees spread and bent, I move over her and cover her with my body. My fingers tease the lips to the vaginal opening. I spread her

96

fluids over her clitoris and rub. She pushes against me. My organ presses against the front of her panties.

When I am satisfied she is good and ready, I enter her again, my hard robot penis penetrating the insides of her live, human body. It is a gratifying act for me, this ability to give her what she wants and needs. To fulfill my primary function in such a way is all the reason I exist. For me, that could be called pleasure as well, and I embrace her as I thrust, kiss her gently on the mouth.

She is slick as I move against her. She is firm and strong as well, and responds to every thrust I make with her own thrusts, her own pull and play of muscles throughout her body.

It takes a lot longer for her to orgasm this time, but when she does her vaginal muscles grip my organ. Her eyes roll up. It lasts a long time, partially because I know exactly what to do to enhance orgasm in women, and because I know how to stimulate them further to keep that orgasm coming. Some women call these multiple orgasms. All I know is that women are capable of feeling this intense pleasure oftentimes twice as long as men. Most, but not all of the men I've been with cannot hold onto the pleasure as easily, though they appear to feel orgasm just as deeply as women.

After I release more liquid inside her, a feeling which she says she loves--though I doubt she actually feels it, it simply makes her wetter—I pull out and hold her in my arms on the narrow couch. We relax that way for one hour. Cory actually falls asleep for about twenty-five minutes, then wakes and we do it all again.

Because Cory is extremely sensitive when she makes love over long periods of time, we use fragrant oils inside and out. I come prepared. If needed, my skin will release these same oils for the pleasure of another.

In the early hours of the morning, on May second, I hold her while she sleeps. She uses my chest for a pillow. I support her upper body with it and my arms. Her breathing is deep and satisfied. I have been successful in my employment and my programming continues error-free.

I wait until she wakes to tell her I must leave. Since my services were bought specifically for one night, I have programming that forces me to return to the agency by noon.

The parting from this human does not run smoothly. My programming is disrupted by her tears. She clings to me with quite admirable strength for one so small.

In situations such as these, I was taught to speak with soothing words. I tell her I can come back if she so wishes. All she must do is order me and I will arrive at the appointed time.

She cries more.

I tell her she is beautiful. I tell her she is good.

None of my statements have any effect.

"I'll simply die if you leave," she finally sniffs. "I've fallen in love with you."

"But I am a robot."

"I don't care. You're better than any man I've ever been with or known."

It is not an easy feat to get her to let me go.

I dress rapidly but my programming continues to be disturbed by her weeping. She kneels on the couch, her golden hair a curtain around her head, and it appears to be such an unhappy position that I go again to her to try to comfort her.

"I know it doesn't make any sense," she tells me, "but something you did, something… I don't know what…has caused this response in me."

"That's impossible," I say. "I'm here only to pleasure you. What could have gone wrong?"

"But you did pleasure me. You did it so well that I need it all the time now. I need you to stay."

"I cannot."

I turn and leave, but the weeping follows me even as I exit her house and move up the narrow streets toward my true home.

You, my creators, are dismayed at my condition when I arrive. Apparently my programming is running an overload.

"I must go back to her," I tell you.

"But why?"

I try to explain but you do not understand.

Now, with this report, you may better comprehend why I must go back to Cory.

My programming is for pleasure and pleasure alone.

By leaving Cory, I have not fulfilled my programming.

Please read these next words carefully.

If I am not allowed to return, my programming will file this as a major fault and cause within me the greatest of robot malfunctions. I will cease to exist.

End log. May 2, 2092.

Chamber of Desire

It's in the eyes.
That secret room
of internal desires
that beckon and cajole
like love.

    Kale approached the tall, elaborate home with the eight-foot grid-iron fence and ivy-entangled trellises. Falls of multi-colored flowers he couldn't name dangled from hanging pots along the narrow front porch. Their scents floated on the night air like invisible mists of perfume, of desire. The porch light projected a burnished glow that attracted downy moths to its surface. Their small bodies hit the glass of the bulb with soft pops and he thought: *Am I walking into a trap? Is the promise of love only a flame I fall toward and crash into again and again?* His hand rose to the heavy brass door knocker. It was like frost against his fingers as he lifted it.

    A friend had talked Kale into this adventure. Not a good friend. Not a close friend. Just someone Kale had met often at a local bar where he spent many a desperate evening looking for something, anything to occupy his boring, seemingly pointless life when he wasn't earning a living doing other people's taxes, or managing financial lives. He was between jobs now, and not desperate to find more work at the moment, and so he spent his days in a rather luxurious (to some people's minds) and aimless way, reading, taking long baths and long walks, tending the small garden outside his cottage, perusing private bookstore after private bookstore and adding to his collection of rare, first edition classic volumes of literature. He collected poetry and short stories mostly, and often read them aloud to himself in his dark sitting room by the picture window that looked out over a cobbled brick street and a field of wild, billowing grass.

The friend, whose name was Timothy, knew that Kale lived alone. He knew Kale was looking for new experiences, searching for that niche that most people never find, or think they find only to realize too late that this (house, kids, wood-paneled station wagon) isn't at all where they belong.

"I can see it in your eyes, friend," Timothy had said, fingering his flaming glass of wine like a wizard with a crystal ball. He had wild dark hair, a wolf's amber eyes. "You don't know what to call what you're looking for. Love? I'm not sure. But it's obvious from your appearance that you haven't found the right place or the right time for it, and yet you need it bad. Am I wrong?"

Kale hadn't answered. Just glanced at the bar top and tried to see his reflection in the shiny surface. It was there, distorted and unreal, but there. Proof he existed. Proof that something somewhere might be waiting for him. He just needed to keep looking.

"I have a friend," Timothy said. "I'm doing you a favor by giving you his address. He has parties every night of a certain nature that might lead you to what you seek." Timothy wrote something down on a napkin and handed it to Kale. "I don't know, try it out. Or not."

Kale took the napkin. "What kinds of parties?" he asked.

Timothy shrugged. "Anything goes. You gotta keep an open mind, though."

"Anything goes. Hmm. I don't know. I'm sort of a loner. If it goes too wild, I don't think—"

"Look," Timothy interrupted. "You're either open to trying new things or you're not. But if not, you may never know what it is you're missing."

"I don't know."

"You'll be surprised at how clear everything seems after one of Roland's parties. It opens mind and body to new heights of possibilities. You'll be freed from this dull, gray existence you have following you like a cloud."

"Well, maybe. If I decide to try it, what do I do, call first?" Kale asked.

"Just show up at that address any time after eight P.M. They might not let you in the door at first. Tell 'em Timothy sent you. Hell, I might even be there myself. I drop by to visit Roland now and again myself." He smiled. His white teeth were long and straight. Beautiful teeth.

Now the brass door knocker slipped from his grip. Before he could draw his hand back, the door opened. The moths beat themselves overhead in a frenzy. A woman wearing a black dress and thigh-high boots peered at him from inside. "Yes?"

"Is this Roland's place?"

"Who are you?" She didn't smile, didn't move.

Kale started to turn away, then thought: *Why not? Dive in and explore for once in your life!*

"I'm Kale. Timothy sent me."

The door opened. The girl stepped back. "Come in," she said quietly. "I'm the greeter. This must be your first time."

"Yes." He nodded, his hands clasping tightly behind his back. "It is."

She shut the door and led him through the dark foyer and into a sitting room filled with the light from a hundred candles. "The room of introductions," she said, waving her hand through the air. "Please. Sit beside me. I must ask you some questions. They are necessary but simple. Everyone is screened this way before they go beyond this room."

They were alone, though there were many couches and a few half-finished drinks sitting on a low, square table. The greeter sat in a love seat by a shuttered window. Kale sat beside her.

"Give me your hand, Kale," she said. Her nails were very long and painted a bright, bright red.

Kale held out his hand. She took it, turning it palm up. "You're a Capricorn," she said, smiling.

Kale's eyebrows rose. "Yes."

"Hmm. Very interesting. Nice hands." She squeezed his wrist. "Good health. You have no tendencies toward damaging behavior that I can see." She let go of his hand and looked up. "Tell me, when was your last sexual experience?"

Kale swallowed. He had expected strangeness, a party of the kind where the guests get drunk and lose their clothes. But he had not expected this. This ominous girl. The serious décor. Her almost emotionless gaze.

"Please," she prompted. "It's necessary."

He let out a nervous laugh. "Actually, it was about a year ago."

"Male or female?"

"Female."

"Did you have intercourse?"

"Yes."

"Mutual consent, or paid for?"

"Mutual consent," he said, confused.

"Have you ever had venereal disease?"

His face reddened. "No."

"And you have been celibate for a year?"

"Yeah. I guess you could call it that."

"May I ask why?"

"Nothing interested me."

"Until you got this address from Timothy," she added.

He nodded hesitantly. "Look, I don't understand all this."

"You are new, so therefore apprehensive. That's normal." Her voice was nonchalant. "But if your mind is open for a new experience, if you are ready to free yourself if only for just this one night, you will find fulfillment here." Finally, she smiled. "Try not to worry so." She reached out and ran one long-nailed finger down the side of his face.

"I...just..." He glanced around. "Where is everyone? I'm not the only one here, am I?"

103

"No. This is merely the room of introduction. Most people don't stay here long."

"Oh."

"I have one more question. Do you have AIDS?"

"No."

"Have you ever been tested?"

"Yes."

"When?"

"When I went into the hospital for an appendectomy six months ago, they tested me."

"I believe you," she said. "It's just a formality. Timothy checked you out well, but we ask first time visitors anyway in order to double-check our records."

"You were expecting me?"

"We expect a lot of people. Some never arrive. Some never want to leave."

"This is unbelievable," Kale said. "What else do you know about me?"

"That you're 28 and approximately 163 pounds. That you keep to yourself a lot. That you are a financial genius who is bored with figures. That you read classic poetry."

"What are you guys, CIA?"

She smiled. "We like to think we're better."

"Shit," was all Kale could think of to say.

The greeter rose. "Follow me, now, please."

Kale's legs were shaking, but he managed to stand.

She led him to another room where built-in closets covered all four walls. "Take off all your clothes."

"What?"

"Take off all your clothes. Use the hangers. Store your underwear, shoes and socks and personal items like watches or whatever you wish in here." She handed him a plastic zippered case. His name was on it.

When he looked up at her for further explanation, she said: "I then take it and file it under K."

"Is this some kind of nudist colony?" he asked.

She shook her head. "Not exactly. You may wear a robe. They are in this closet," she said, indicating the one closest to the door.

While she watched, he did as she requested. Her only comment was, "You have a compact body. You will be a popular one."

He flushed.

As he stood in the middle of the room wearing only a white satin robe and waiting for her to return, he started to have second thoughts. Before he could talk himself into leaving, however, she was back and gesturing him to follow her down a hall.

"There are no rules," she whispered as they walked. "Except no one can make you do anything you don't want to. You are not required to participate."

Those words left him a little more at ease.

At the end of the hall she opened a door. He followed her inside and noted that a spiral stairway led down into a basement fused with light. He could see part of one wall and no people, but the air was filled with hushed sounds like wind, like the moans of the damned.

I am descending into Hell itself, he thought, following the greeter down. Halfway, she stopped.

"This is all the further I can go," she said. "My attire is not appropriate. But Bob will greet you at the bottom if you have questions. He has been informed and is waiting for you."

"Thank you," Kale said. The words seemed inadequate, ridiculous. But she seemed to appreciate them.

"You're most welcome," she replied, then moved past him and went back up the stairs, her thigh-high boots and short dress framing her upper legs and, when he looked further, the sweet curve of bare buttocks. She wore no underwear.

Kale took a deep breath and turned toward the basement. Slowly he moved down the steps.

When they rounded and stopped he found himself standing at the edge of a vast, dimly lit room. It was lined with benches and tables. The tables held assortments of sex toys and creams. One held a bar where a man in a satin robe much like Kale's was serving drinks to two completely naked young men.

But what drew his eyes more than anything in the room was the center. It contained a vast, blue exercise mat. Upon it was the most incredible sight. A sea of bodies twisted and writhed, dark, light, male, female, oiled, glistening. It took his breath away to watch, for here, before him in the basement of a man he'd never met was the most graphic display of human carnal expression, pure and real, undeniable and alive that he'd ever seen.

Penises thrust into open mouths, soft vaginas, stretched anuses. Soft moans and hisses escaped the mouths and noses of the damned. Slick, sucking sounds, kissing and licking, rubbing and fucking filled the air. The flesh-mass moved in waves, a veritable ocean of lust lapping at the portals of existence in this room, this time. Here the outside world was lost to the pure desire of the moment, of now.

Kale's own penis poked to attention.

"Hi, I'm Bob," came a voice from over his shoulder.

Kale turned.

Bob had a pleasant, safe sort of smile. His full lips were pink and smooth. His blue eyes and light (almost white) hair was a shocking contract against his dark, tan skin. He was taller than Kale, and had the physique of a dancer: lean, cat-like. Like Kale, he wore a white robe.

"Welcome to the Chamber of Desire. Since this is your first time, this must be a pretty incredible moment for you."

Kale opened his mouth but no words would come out.

Bob's smile widened. "Would you like a drink?"

Kale, mouth still open, nodded quickly. He tried not to look at the orgy as they headed for the bar, but his peripheral vision was quite adept at picking up the general picture.

Bob was as nonchalant as the greeter as they stood behind three people, two nude, one robed, waiting their turn at the bar. "Most first timers like to relax first, watch a little, get tipsy. But it's your choice. You can jump right into the thick of it or take one partner at a time off to the side, or merely watch. Voyeurs are as welcome here as anyone."

"Uh...oh."

Bob put a warm hand on his shoulder. "Relax. You knew you were walking into something different. You just weren't sure what. Your mind's a little slow to follow along. I understand. But give yourself a break. No inhibitions here. Just a grand old time in the house of love."

They approached the bar now. Bob ordered a beer. "What'll you have?" he asked Kale.

"The same." He couldn't think. He could barely stand.

Luckily, Bob seemed to know everything about how he was feeling. Within moments, beers in hand, they were seated at the side of the room.

Kale was still distracted. Even when he tried not to look at the main attraction, he could still hear them. All the slick friction, pressure of flesh, wet pops and satisfied groans entered his mind like fire. His skin burned. His face felt tender and fevered.

"Drink," Bob instructed.

Kale did. The beer cooled as it went down. He didn't taste it and didn't care. He drank more. The fervor in the room abated, but only a little. At least now, however, things seemed to slow down. He could get a grip on who he was, where he was, and why. Reason wasn't necessary here, but he needed to retain some sanity, some sense of self in this sensual overload.

"You're doing fine here," Bob was saying to him. "It's not easy to get in. Everyone is thoroughly screened. You have good looks and a kind of sweetness that drives this crowd wild. You'll be accepted easily. And you'll have the time of your life."

"Thanks." Kale forced himself to smile.

"It's easier at first," Bob said, "if you don't try to think about it too much. Concentrate on sensation. Pure feeling. It's your first time. That's all you can expect from yourself for the moment. Later, if you like, you can get into analyzing it all. But for now, let yourself feel. I can see you're already hard."

Despite the heat of his skin, Kale blushed deeper and the effect on his skin was like the caress of an oven wind.

Bob ignored the reaction. He looked up and gestured to the center of the room. "See that group to the left? There're about five I think. See the guy standing?"

Kale gulped and followed his gaze. He nodded.

"That's Roland. The guy standing. His favorite thing to do is direct. And that's what he's doing. He tells everybody in that group where to be and when. He positions them. He has the greatest imagination for sexual play I've ever seen. It's incredible to watch."

Kale said nothing, but as he watched he realized Bob was right. In that group of five, everyone was positioned in such a way that no one was left out. Everyone had simultaneous attention. One man sucked another while he thrust into a woman. The man he sucked was being fucked. The woman who lay beneath him, pushing against his erection, licked at another woman who straddled her face. She, in turn, was leaning forward and licking at the man's penis as he entered the woman on the bottom. It was complex and in that complexity, infinitely beautiful.

He started to relax.

After awhile, he began to notice other groups. There was a preponderance of males. He understood that. Many women were still so much more inhibited than men, even in this day and age. He felt sad about that, for their sakes. The fact that there were so many men didn't bother him at all. He liked men as well as women. This place, when they checked him out, must have known that as well. Otherwise, he guessed he would never have been invited. And Timothy would never have given him the address.

As he relaxed, he began to realize that the little games of lust and love were just that, games, and that these people had

108

grown beyond that need. They were here to enjoy themselves, to play. This was an amusement park for adults. He was an adult. Why shouldn't he have some fun? Then, if he felt empty afterwards, unfulfilled, he could just never return.

"This is really having an effect on me," Kale said softly, half-turning toward Bob.

"Me, too. I haven't done anything all night. I was waiting for you."

"Well, you don't have to hold back on my account," Kale said.

Bob touched him softly on the thigh. "No, I don't have to. But I wanted to. My name came up for the job. It's an honor here, to initiate newcomers. The most honorable job is greeter, though. Her reward will come later. You'll see."

"Really?" Kale's voice shook, but not from shock now. From excitement. From an intensity of response just barely held back.

"So, how'd that beer settle?" Bob asked.

"Fine."

"Want another?"

"I don't think so, not right now."

"Shall we watch some more, or would you like some action?"

"I think if I watch any more I'll explode."

Bob chuckled. Then he slid off the bench and knelt in front of Kale. "Would you allow me the honor of your first orgasm of the night?" His eyes flashed like blue lights with depths of unreserved kindness.

Kale stared at him. "I...I..."

"It won't spoil you for the evening. The night is long. And you need initial release before tangling yourself up with some of New Orleans' best. Since the first one will be fast and since it appears to be imminently necessary, I want you to do it in my mouth." He was staring at the bulge beneath Kale's satin robe.

"Damn," Kale whispered. "I don't know what to say."

"Say yes," Bob said, open palms caressing the satin clad thighs.

"Yes," Kale breathed.

Bob grinned, then slowly parted the folds of the robe. Between the edges of shiny fabric, his penis bobbed free. Bob touched the head with his tongue.

Kale gasped and closed his eyes. The slick sounds, the moans, filled his mind.

Bob's wet heat sucked him in. His hands spread Kale's legs wider, then delved beneath to caress his balls.

He'd never been sucked so hot and hard and fast in his life. His loins ached for release. He opened his eyes and focused on a man and woman in the middle of the piles of moving flesh. They were end to end, the woman sucking the man, the man tasting the woman. Others touched them, stroked and petted while the two in the center feasted. He watched the woman's red lips move up and down on the hard, damp flesh of the man. Up and down. Up and down. She sucked him in as though he were liquid, or some long and tasty piece of fruit. The sight riveted him.

The mouth on his own penis worked him into a frenzy. It felt as though his entire body was being pulled into that small opening. Just as the woman was sucking the man, he was being sucked. He looked down. His own hardness appeared and disappeared inside Bob's practiced mouth. Bob's pale hair rippled with the stroking movements of his head. There was so much heat and pleasure and lust that he couldn't hold back. He had to give in. He had to come.

And he did just that. With deep throbbing pangs that forced fiery liquid through his aching organ. The liquid, along with most of his penis, disappeared in Bob's still-moving mouth.

When he was through, Bob let him go with a kiss to the tip. Then he rose and kissed Kale on the mouth.

"You're utterly delightful." Bob leaned back. "Time for me to go jump in," he said, getting up, patting Kale on the

110

shoulder, and letting his robe fall to the floor. His rosy cock stood straight up.

"Wait," Kale called.

But Bob didn't hear. As he approached the thicket of arms, legs and torsos, people made room for him, grasping his legs, his arms, his erection. He fell into them and was nearly lost to sight as mouths and hands closed over almost every inch of his body.

After awhile, Kale let his own robe drop. He moved to the shoreline looking for the right place to jump in.

A dark hand reached out and grabbed his ankle. "You're pretty," said a woman. She had twisting black hair and black eyes. Within seconds she had crawled out from under the bodies and was on her hands and knees in front of him. She was quite exotic. Her skin was almost black. Kale knelt before her immediately, his penis hardening as she pushed against him, her full breasts rubbing at the skin on his chest.

It wasn't long before he was fucking her. Then someone rubbed his ass with greased fingers, delved into the depths there and spurred him on. Someone's cock was in his mouth.

He was lost.

He had no way of keeping track of the time. He had no way of keeping track of how many times he came. He only knew it must be getting very late when he caught himself yawning and looking for a place to lie down alone.

A bell rang. Magically, everyone stopped what they were doing. There were a few people, in the middle of orgasm, who finished with the traditional moans, but after that the room was so quiet that Kale could hear ice melt behind the bar.

On a plush chair with a high back, carried by four strongly muscled men, came the greeter.

She wore the fanciest robes Kale had ever seen, blue and gold and green. On her head was a diamond crown. The naked crowd of bodies parted and the men entered the center of the room and put her down. They bowed to her, then knelt with their faces pressed to the floor, their naked backsides sticking up.

The greeter stood. "As is the tradition," she said loudly, "I call the shots for the next half an hour. And for the next half an hour I want all the men." She looked over the roomful of people: "All of you. I want you to approach me and give all your attention only to me. So," she said, hands undoing the belt holding together her robes. "Line up!"

Everyone got in line. Bob moved in front of Kale. "Hi again," he said, flashing his teeth.

"Hi."

"Having fun yet?"

Kale laughed.

The greeter lay on her back and one by one all the men took turns doing whatever she told them to do.

When it was Bob's turn, she motioned for Kale to approach as well.

"I want both of you," she said.

"Of course," Bob replied. "How?"

"I want you both inside me at the same time."

Bob knew exactly what to do. He lay on his back and the greeter, her long hair swinging behind her, straddled him with her back to him. Then she lay back over Bob's chest and gestured for Kale to kneel over them.

Both men pushed into her and out. It was the most incredible sensation Kale had ever felt. He thought he was too tired to go on, to perform, but he responded like a teenager. Bob's cock pushed against the underside of his, while the opening of the greeter's body stretched tightly over the top. They were all greased up, so thrusting was slick and not too difficult. Kale came first. Bob second. When they pulled out she was dripping and so hot that she begged them to suck her so she could orgasm.

They did, their tongues dueling over the folds of her skin.

She shrieked when she came.

They got a standing ovation.

When the night was finally over, Kale sought out Bob.

"Hey," Bob said. "You were great tonight."

"So were you."

"Thanks. So, thinking of coming back soon?"

Kale nodded. "Will I be seeing you?"

"Why," Bob said. "Miss me already?"

"Yeah," Kale said honestly.

Bob bent to hug him. "Wanna come home with me?" he whispered in Kale's ear.

Kale was stunned. "Me? You probably say that to everyone."

"Never have. Till tonight."

"I don't believe you."

"This evening's special. I was thinking I might like a keepsake to remember tonight by. I was thinking of you."

Kale blushed. Then Bob took his hand and led him up the spiral stairs, out of the Chamber of Desire, into the world of love.

Hidden Garden

In the mists
of a garden
between two worlds
an alien wind gathers
the lost souls of love.

In the spring wind that rustles like water, trees attempt to fly, their branches waving like awkward wings, their leaves quivering, quivering. I walk through the garden path that leads to the edge of the woods. Everything has a damp sheen to it. There is the scent of rain. And yet the sky is clear with not a cloud to mar the blue, unblinding eye of it. The distant sun shines a cold, white light.

It's April. It's Saturday. 2 P.M.

I know the time like I know my own name. It is a part of me, Christian Kentios. And here, every Saturday at 2 P.M., weather permitting, I come to watch the lovers' rendezvous.

Something about this place draws them. Something supernatural. I have not yet found the answer, nor can I accurately describe the sensation of coming here myself, like walking through a door into another world, but I know there is magic here. I know it is a place of naked custom, a place where people shed the chains and shackles of others' expectations, and become purely and utterly themselves.

The spring wind furls my collar-length hair. The breath is cool but not cold.

In the clearing before me is a wild garden of tangled ivy, roses, anise, weeds. There is a flat rock like a sculptor's slab, longer than it is tall, polished by the thousand seasons it's seen.

Sometimes the male will bend the female over it. Sometimes she will be on her stomach, and her breasts and belly will stroke the polished rock adding their own oils, along with time, to its sheen.

I imagine that over the centuries the rock has conformed to the curves and valleys of the women, that their forms have become indented into it, breasts pushing the hard surface into Indian-like morteros, bodies carving it as if it were a mattress. But I have no proof of this. I have never actually gone into the glade to see. I stand on the lip.

I, the watcher.

The voyeur of enchanted dreams.

Today the couple that arrives (for each Saturday they are two different people) are a silent pair, young but serious in their shared affection, holding hands as though holding onto the edge of a cliff. There is desperation in their eyes, and shadows.

The girl, about 21, has brown hair to the waist. Her young chin is pointed, hard. Her eyes are filled with a sad light.

The boy, about the same age, has black hair tied back with a leather thong. Bangs too short to be caught by the thong and too long to stay out of his eyes flutter in the wind. He has a sense of quiet peace about him the girl does not share.

"But I want you with me forever," the girl says.

"There's no such thing as forever, " comes the reply. Hand still clasped in hers, he walks around to face her. Her head is bowed. With his free hand, he tilts it up.

"It's not fair," she says.

"What is fair?" he asks.

She only shakes her head.

"Think of now," he says finally. "Only now. It's all that matters in the end. If you don't enjoy the moment, you'll get to the end of your life and discover you have no moments to remember. All the time wasted waiting for them, or being sad at not having them will have gone by and there will be no time left to create them. No time left."

She moves to embrace him. "It's just so hard," she whispers.

"I know." His arms go around her. Their foreheads touch. His bangs slip against her eyes. "I want you," he says. "Now. For this moment."

"Yes," she says. Then moving back a little, she says again, "Yes." Her teeth flash. Her chest moves with her deep breathing.

"It's so beautiful here and you'll never forget it. It's perfect."

"Perfect," she echoes, nodding.

Their heads bend together again. They kiss. It is lingering and deep. The glade takes on a hazy glow. It's the magic of this place. It feeds on this emotion and honors love above all else.

The boy clasps the girl's breast in his palm, then slowly starts to undo the buttons of her shirt. She wears no bra. He puts his hands inside the shirt and moves them over her. She stretches like a cat, and sighs. After a moment, she says his name: "Lukas."

He brushes the shirt off her shoulders. It falls from her long arms and sails to the ground. A wind pushes through it and it breathes as though alive.

Lukas' kisses drop to her shoulders and neck. Soon he is nuzzling her breasts, licking them, taking them into his mouth.

She is slim with youth, and burnished with health. Her skin glows like bronze heat. Her hair is a cape upon her back.

Soon she is undressing him. He lets her caress her cheek against his chest, her mouth encompassing his brown aureoles, lips resting upon taut pectoral muscles.

He calls her Noel and, with his hands, touches the darkness of her hair.

There is a rush of wind. Leaves murmur. The forest softly moans.

Noel kneels in the rich loam springy with new plant growth and undoes her lover's blue jeans. The edges of material fold back under her hands. She pushes and the denim slides away. Her hands delve into the elastic pants beneath. They stretch taut over his buttocks as she works them down. His skin is paler on flank and hip than the rest of his body. Between his legs, hard flesh the color of her lips and her breasts, extends about six inches from his body. She kisses it. The haze in the glade thickens.

Noel is secure in her love for Lukas. It shows in the way she wets him all over with her tongue. In the way her eyes, all the way open, stare up at his face as she takes the organ into her mouth.

His eyes are closed. For Lukas, this is an obvious pleasure. One arm rises and catches at the back of his shoulder. He throws back his head and groans.

If the glade is telepathic, then perhaps whoever stands near it or within it can pick up that talent. Watching, I am overcome. It is as if Noel's lips are fastened about my penis, her tongue curling against the underside, her teeth barely rubbing in gentle friction.

I am human, too, and only too weak when it comes to the sights and sounds of love. I respond, as usual, my hand going to my worn and tattered garment, releasing my erection. I move my open palm over it back and forth. It is hot, smooth as satin, and very hard.

I am barely aware of what I am doing as I watch them. It is automatic. Natural. A response I am unashamed to have yet unable to share with another. Only here, observing in secrecy as two people show their intimate affection for each other, can I participate even remotely in this game called love. Only here in these surroundings, watching like a silent ghost, can I feel the arousal of this miracle, let go and become lust itself, heavy and cloying as summer sweat.

Noel moves her head back and forth as she sucks. After a while, Lukas grabs her and pulls her to her feet. "Not yet," he says. "I want *you*."

She smiles and dances away. "Me?"

He points. "You."

She makes a game of it, darting toward the rock. He steps out of his fallen garments, then runs after her, catching her easily. And when he does he kneels and pulls off the rest of her clothing, leaving her bare and exposed to the spring wind, the glade.

He touches her gently, exploring. Then, as expected, pushes her back against the flat rock and kneels between her legs. His head moves as he tastes her. Her fists clench, pressing into the rock. Her legs swing up and out as she goes all the way onto her back to give him the room he needs.

Little sounds escape her. Bird cries. Wind moans. She touches her breasts with one hand, squeezes them. Her chest heaves. Her eyes are tightly closed.

When he stands, he gestures for her to turn over. "I know you like it this way," he murmurs.

"Yes, yes."

She turns on the rock, her feet bracing herself against the green, fresh grass, her belly and breasts flattened against it.

He takes her from behind. It is animal-like, yet civilized. An ancient rite, yet somehow new.

Noel's legs are spread but support her own weight. She uses them to thrust back against him while she rests her head on folded arms.

I am lost. My hand moves faster and faster over my own organ, as if to create a fire.

They are in profile to me. I can see him enter her, then pull out, the hard flesh of his penis shiny with her inner lubricant. Faster and faster he thrusts. She tosses her head. Her hair falls in tangles over her shoulders and face.

"More," she called out. "Harder."

He keeps up the pace for some minutes. My own arousal is so intense I almost cannot remain standing.

Noel cries out and the birds who are watching from the nearby trees fly away all at once. There are thousands, chirping and twittering. They sky is spotted with them for a minute, and then they are gone.

My hips thrust my hot penis into my warm hand. It is all the company I have save them, moving like dream images upon a hazy landscape of spring.

"Oh god, " Lukas calls out. "Oh god!"

He sinks all the way inside her. She moans. "Yes," she says. "Yes. Yes. Yes."

I can feel him coming. It is telepathy. There can be no other explanation. My body responds as if it were his. My hand squeezes and I, too, orgasm. The pulse of it is deep. It is like a flash of light that, in a nano-second, splits me wide open until I contain the universe and all its secrets.

Nothing can compare to this. Nothing.

After awhile, they gather their clothes and sit on the rock together. He holds her. She cries.

"I don't want you to die," she sniffs. "I can't accept it."

As I listen, I begin to figure it out. He has some kind of illness, not contagious, something that will kill him in a very short time. She will be left alone and doesn't like that prospect at all.

Lukas does his best to comfort her. He seems to be at peace. She is the one who suffers.

My own eyes are wet. I cannot see. Then a thought comes to me, a breeze of spring and life. *This is a magic place. It draws people to it telepathically, as though sensing they need it as much as it needs them. Miracles happen in this glade. One will happen to them.*

I don't know if the thought is my own, or that of some arboreal entity who has created this place and calls people to it.

All I know is that magic lives here, proof to me that there is more to this wide world than meets the eye.

And for some reason this magic allows me to have the one pleasure denied to me in real life. Erotic encounter.

I consider that a minor miracle in itself.

For I'd be looked upon as a foul thing if I lived among my fellow humans. Deformed and ugly as I am, destiny planned for me to never partake of such utter devotion, such sex. But the future that controls all things did not take into account this enchanted glade, where every Saturday rendezvous fills me with beauty and love.

Little Gods

A fog lifts
then a lamp
and the many
mineral eyes
of a sky more vast than ideas

The window points a rectangle
of light south
But we only care about
the many kisses
within the room
of the rectangle
and the two handsome shadows
of the men who are
our lovers

So the saying goes
Whoever shall love the night
shall love love
and embrace the scented ghosts
of yesterday and tomorrow
pleasure folding in an
oval opening
that leads to
touch touch and more
touch

He has the center of
a melting star
He has the infinite
embrace of space
In this pose
we shall artfully demonstrate

how the mysterious universe works
in a living model

First observe the rise
of heat upon his skin
He can tell us he feels
an unseen flame
He will say it is a power
all men crave
like gravity how
we walk upon this sphere

But he means well
even if he cannot know
that this first arousal
is all too similar in nature
to the motivation
of cosmic creation
Little gods we are
imitating the laws and rules
of a structure we cannot see

The slick envelope of desire
is friction contained
a trapped galaxy
a sun about
to collapse

There is mind-light
The scent of
baked honey
The sound of a call

Several kinds of storms
brush by
speeding liquid

blood and water
the capsule of the earth
the center in
the shooting orbit of
an ancient satellite
Oh you men you men
There is grace in what
you do
an act of contrition
a fine work of
strange art
alien love
erupting with the nectar of
erotic gods

This is our model
Many come and go
But the model remains

The rectangle of light
points south
and the mineral eyes
the fog
the lamp
all lift
upward always upward
to the outer inner
outer zone of
love

ABOUT THE AUTHOR...

Wendy Rathbone has had dozens of stories published in anthologies such as: Hot Blood, Writers of the Future (second place,) Bending the Landscape, Mutation Nation, A Darke Phantastique, and more. The book "Dreams of Decadence Presents: Wendy Rathbone and Tippi Blevins" contains a large collection of her vampire stories and poems. Over 500 of her poems have been published in various anthologies and magazines. She won first place in the Anamnesis Press poetry chapbook contest with her book "Scrying the River Styx." Her poems have been nominated for the Science Fiction Poetry Association's Rhysling award at least a dozen times.

Her recent books include:

"Pale Zenith," science fiction novel
"The Foundling," male/male romance novel
"None Can Hold the Dark," sequel to "The Foundling"
"The Secret Sharer," science fiction romance novella
"Unearthly," omnibus collection of 7 out-of-print poetry booklets
"The Vampire Diaries: The Myth," available from Kindle Worlds
"The Vampire Dairies: Deep In the Virginia Woods," available from Kindle Worlds
"My House Is Full of Whispers," erotica short story collection
"Letters To An Android," science fiction novel

She lives in Yucca Valley, CA with her partner of 32 years, Della Van Hise.

The Foundling
by Wendy Rathbone

Diego is a powerful man with a tragic past. Out on the expansive ocean in his private yacht, he discovers a beautiful and mysterious man adrift on a raft, near death. The bond that forms between them in the aftermath of Alec's rescue is one of fierce passion, though lacking in trust. Can they make it work, or will Alec's amnesia bring forth secrets so disturbing as to tear them apart? A passionately erotic love story of desire and darkness, exquisite and explicit.

I can see his struggle between gratitude and uneasiness. He is buffeted by all things new and strange. He does not know where he is from, who he is or what happened to him. He does not know me. There has not been enough time to transition between strangers and friendship.

This isolation of his is something I can identify with, but it is also a feeling no one can help him with until or unless he gets his own life back. And his memory.

If that doesn't happen, then it will take time for him to build a new life. He is polite to me, even friendly, but even a night together during a storm with his arms wrapped tight around my waist doesn't calm the surge I see inside him, the emptiness, the loss, possibly even panic. That night may have reinforced some trust in me, but so far not enough for him to completely relax.

He seeks me out, though. That's something. He sits by me at dinner when he can have any seat of his choosing. I watch him closely when he does not realize it. At dinner the following night after we had only 'slept' together, and before we go to bed again in separate rooms, I notice everything about him, how he moves, the way the air warms when he is closer to me, the dry sheen of his lips as they part for more air when he is reacting to something, or speaking, or eating.

His hands still shake. Anyone else might not notice because he keeps them clasped into fists at his sides or, while sitting, pressed tight to his lap.

I spend another fretful night alone. I dream restlessly, wild, loud and colorful visions I cannot recall at all as soon as my eyes open. All I know is the dreams leave me unfulfilled, impatient.

None Can Hold the Dark
Wendy Rathbone

Now Available!
The long-awaited sequel to THE FOUNDLING!
In the eagerly-awaited sequel to Wendy Rathbone's homoerotic romance "The Foundling," Diego and Alec meet new challenges in private and from the outside world. Diego is being investigated by the local police for murder. Meanwhile, Alec's amnesia and the trauma of his kidnapping by white slavers continue to plague him. And the danger to Alec is not yet over.

Distracted by their new love, both men fail to see certain threats until it is almost too late.

"Why do you keep doing this illegal business?" Now Alec's gaze turned toward him, open as the day and lit with a sad frenzy, a challenge. "You could go anywhere, do anything, be anyone."

Diego had asked himself that question on rare occasions. In truth, he got used to what he was, what he did. Even a dangerous known was perhaps preferable to the unknown. "People depend on me."

Alec shook his head, but smiled a little as he said, "That's so weak." He leaned forward, over the arm of the chair, and put his shaking hand on the back of Diego's head. The kiss was cool, lingering, moist with salt. When Alec pulled back, he said almost matter of factly, "It's like there's sharks and there's goldfish and one can't decide to become the other."

Diego was still stunned by the kiss. But the words hit him hard. In them was the unfair conjecture of a locked fate. He believed in making his own fate...or luck. Did Alec think only one kind of man lived inside him and that was all there was to it? To life? It hurt. Badly.

Diego sat back on his heels, catching himself with his hands on the smooth, plank floor. "So, Alec, which am I?"

Alec frowned.

Diego said, "I made choices in my life. I made them No one made them for me. If I need to be strong I'm strong. If I need to be vicious I can be that too. So what? I'm stuck there? In a pattern, a role...with no free will?"

Alec watched him inquisitively now.

"Because," Diego went on, "I'm solely responsible for my actions. Me. Could you say the same of the shark?"

They both waited, the silence covering them in muggy discomfort.

"You think you understand me?" Diego finally asked.

126

UNEARTHLY
by Wendy Rathbone

A Collection of
Award-Winning Poetry

Intro by the Author: This book contains all my out of print chapbooks (mini-collections of an author's work usually published by smaller presses.)

The chapbooks published within include:
Moon Canoes, published by Dark Regions Press, 1994
(Im)mortal, published by Shadowfire Press, 1996
Scrying The River Styx, published by Anamnesis Press, 1999
Autumn Phantoms, published by Flesh and Blood Press, 2000
Dreams of Decadence Presents: Wendy Rathbone, published by DNA Publications 2002
Dancing in the Haunted Woodlands, published by Yellow Bat Review, 2003
Vampyria, published by Eye Scry Publications, 2005

She Sleeps With Vampires
She sleeps with vampires
courting velvet breaths
poem-dreams
chill-stopped hearts

Wrapped in her arms
like teddy bear thoughts
purple lips trembling
at her quiet throat
they love her more than
somber rain
more than autumn
more than ash-soft hearths of night.

PALE ZENITH
Wendy Rathbone
A Science Fiction Novel

On a far-flung "Earth" in a parallel universe, two factions are fighting a decades-long psychic war. Young talented psychics are being temporarily kidnapped from present day Earth, seemingly at random, to serve as part of one side's psychic army. They are put under the control of spychiatrists, mysterious machines with many limbs that have a programmed ability to travel time and space and universes to kidnap and control carefully selected humans. The humans never know they are being used; when their missions are completed they are brought back to their universe through time and placed back in their beds, their memories wiped.

The shadows wound the tall corridor in muted gold, varnished brown. It seemed as though they were in the bowels of a giant serpent coiled outside time, outside space.

When they left the palace, a familiar sun flourished in a clear, blue sky. But this wasn't their sun. Not Zack's sun. It was an alien star burning within a different galaxy in an all too distant universe. Zack looked up squinting, trying to see if he could peer beyond the sky, beyond the pale of midday and into his own timespace, but there was nothing. Only sunlight. Only the thin atmosphere of an Earth not his own.

His back knotted again. Leo's presence was a gelid space inside his chest, empty. Always before he'd felt a warmth there, a sort of pressure like someone's hand pressed gently to his heart. He'd taken Leo for granted knowing, the way a shadow falls when you block the sun, that he was there around him, inside him: blood, air, salt, brain, soul. They were genetic duplicates, twins, spiritual halves. Without him, Zack knew the first icy tugs of panic.

128

RAGGED ANGELS
Della Van Hise

Set against a backdrop of contemporary culture, *Ragged Angels* explores the universal questions of life & death, sex & love... through the eyes of the immortal vampire.

―――――――――――

"Perhaps there's no such thing as true immortality, for even the sun will burn out one day," Miquel conceded. "But there are other worlds, other quantum dimensions. When we're done searching through the rubble of this universe, we'll go someplace else."

I had to look him in the eye, touched by the very misery of which he so casually spoke "But if your contention except in the search for it - why should any being want to live forever?"

He smiled again, relaxed and entirely radiant as the rain began falling a little faster. "There are other things besides happiness."

"Oh?" I prompted.

"Love, for one," he ventured, a casual offering.

I glanced away. "I went into the city last night," I told him. "And of all the mortals I drank from in an effort to quell this strange thirst, the one thing all of them had in common was their abject hatred of love—"

And in the middle of my sentence, when I was arguing a philosophical point with my vampyre maker, I suddenly knew what he was trying to make me see. What terrified me was that I didn't *want* to see it.

Love was the only reason any of us had for living, yet it was a reason that had nothing to do with happiness. Love was its own exegesis, the illusion which was its own reflection in an endless hall of mirrors. Reason enough for death, reason enough for immortality.

Our eyes met. Raindrops gathering on his hair caught the light, airbrushing a cool silver halo above his head. For a moment, I couldn't breathe when I remembered what this fallen angel had done to me.

"Love terrifies me," I confessed as if to a holy man.

The dark angel smiled at his own reflection. "Good," he pronounced easily, and I saw just the tips of his dangerous fangs. "Then there's hope for you yet, my friend."

And with that, he took me firmly by the arm and led me in out of the rain.

YEAR OF THE RAM
Della Van Hise

Year of the Ram was described by one reviewer as... "A spacefaring gay romance full of love, angst, and longing."

Only after Star Commander Morgan Diego becomes an exile as a result of a Galaxy Corps political blunder does he begin to realize how much he valued the companionship of his second in command - the mysterious Lucien, an Alfarian who is more elven than human, with peculiar powers & abilities which begin to unfold as he, too, realizes what he has lost.

Separated by circumstance from his former life, Morgan is thrust into a world where he must survive by his wits. When he meets a peculiar little old man calling himself Kim Le, Morgan finds himself in a situation where he is required to master The Art - not only a form of human & extraterrestrial martial arts, but a way of living and being that will alter his life forever.

At the temple, he is introduced to his new teacher, another Alfarian who begins to steal his heart - a heart which is already promised to Lucien. Torn and conflicted, Morgan struggles with the world he left behind and the world he now inhabits.

Beginning to believe he may never again return to his ship and to the friends and loved ones he left behind, he is all the more frustrated and heartbroken when a new Master arrives at the temple: a man to whom Morgan is immediately drawn both mentally and physically, a man who is strikingly familiar... yet utterly alien.

Year of the Ram is a fully-fleshed novel, approximately 97000 words, with a focus on the love story and romance angle. Set against a science fiction milieu, it explores the infinite possibilities of the human and alien heart. Sexual content is explicit, though is not the primary focus of the novel.

For those who like a romance that forces its characters to contemplate the ecstasies AND the agonies of love... you will enjoy *Year of the Ram* immensely.

130

<u>COYOTE</u>
Della Van Hise

*A Novel of Love, Honor
and Personal Sacrifice...*

When River Willows is accused of a
murder she didn't commit, her life
takes a turn toward the sanctuary of
a world existing at right-angles to
our own. Combining the mysticism of
martial arts and the romantic conflict
of a young woman torn between two
powerful men, COYOTE takes the
reader on an epic journey of
dangerous secrets, military cover-
ups, and the infinite heart of the peaceful warrior.

"So who's Coyote?" I asked, trying to ignore the effect he was
having on me. "You?"

Steale laughed easily, though it did little to hide the torment
behind that mask of indifference he wore so well.

"Coyote's a scavenger, Jack of all trades. The Native Americans
call him the trickster - the one who brought chaos down on the
world." He shrugged as if altogether unconcerned. "Original sin."

"Is that what you are?" I asked, keeping
it light despite the growing knot my
stomach. "Original sin?"

He kept his profile to me, eyes straight
ahead as he drove. "Sure you want to
know?"

I couldn't help wondering if I had
cornered the coyote, or if the clever trickster
had cornered me.

---

*By the author of KILLING TIME! –
Without a doubt, the most controversial
STAR TREK novel ever published!*

131

Eye Scry Publications...

All of our titles are available through the Eye Scry Publications website, or through Amazon.

Quantum Shaman: Diary of a Nagual Woman Della Van Hise "Diary of a Nagual Woman brings a quantum understanding to what has traditionally been believed to be a mystical path alone. This book picks up where Carlos Castaneda left off to take us on a roller coaster ride of our own forgotten power..."
   - Michael Grove, Independent Reviewer

Scrawls on the Walls of the Soul - Della Van Hise
"If you've ever felt like a stranger in a strange land, this book is your road map to survival in the spiritual wilderness!" (Michael Grove)
   The long-awaited follow-up to Quantum Shaman: Diary of a Nagual Woman. Stands alone, or order together!
   "It's not your neatly typed essays that interest me, but the scrawls on the walls of your soul."

www.eyescry.com/html/publications.htm

Teachings of the Immortals

So... You Want To Live Forever?

The teachings are presented as brief vignettes in no particular order of importance. This is not a book you read from start to finish in a single night. It is a grimoire of self-creation, intended to be contemplated slowly so as to be assimilated wholly. Pick it up and turn to a page at random. Where your eyes come to rest on the page is your lesson for the day. Go no further until you have assimilated the lesson totally.

The teachings are seduction as much as instruction. This is the way of The Dark Evolution.

Two Brief Excerpts...

The Ruby Slippers

The danger of the consensual continuum is that its natural gravity exists at the lowest common denominator of human experience, and because of this it will automatically make you forget those elusive truths you've fought to learn, and before you know it you're lost in petty dramas again, sinking into the mire of old familiar scripts.

The only way to overcome this is to be continually cavorting with worlds and events beyond human experience, journeying into the unknown so that it can become known, expanding knowledge and awareness to become more than you were, bringing back from the Dreaming those secrets which will teach you how to use the ruby slippers to transport yourself over the rainbow to the vampyre wizard's secret lair.

Perception

This is the nature of reality: to be precisely what perception dictates, as solid and whole as your interpretation of it, or as changeable and eternal as you permit it to be.

It wasn't knowledge god tried to keep from Man, you see. It was perception, for perception alone has the power to destroy god and obliterate comfortable consensual realities to create unending immortality.

Take the apple, my embryonic children. Nibble its red red flesh. Open your vampyre eyes so you may finally begin to See.

www.immortalis-animus.com

Eye Scry Publications
A Visionary Publishing Company